PRESUMED DEAD

by

Dawn Sherwood

For Graham

Acknowledgements

Special thanks go to Jenny Bailey and Audrey McIlvain for their invaluable feedback during the writing of this book. I will be forever indebted to Penny Murison for taking on the arduous task of proof reading and identifying that I really do have a thing about commas!

Chapter 1

Her whole body was rigid with fear. Her sense of smell and sound, completely overwhelmed by the roar of the sea water crashing against the dark, uninviting rocks below. As the wind whipped against her skin, sea-spray stinging her eyes, she caught the faint odour of stale sweat and cigarette smoke. Her feet were now dangerously close to the edge of the cliff, but there was no possibility of moving back. He was right behind her. Tightening the thick, coarse rope with every movement she made. Pulling it tighter and tighter around an already bruised throat. As he reached forward to move her hands away from the makeshift noose, her eyes caught sight of the ring on his finger. She tried to twist around to see his face. To plead with him, why was he doing this? Then suddenly a feeling of falling; blackness........

Annie sat bolt upright in bed. She was gasping for air and her whole body felt damp with sweat. Bonnie slowly raised her head and with tired eyes, gazed quizzically at Annie, while at the same time sniffing the air trying to determine what the faint smell was that her nostrils were picking up. Her owner was evidently not going back to sleep quickly, so, lazily stretching all four of her legs as she rose from the floor, she plopped her head onto Annie's bed hoping for some owner to dog exchange.

Annie tentatively felt her neck. It was tender to the touch and the metallic taste of blood was strong in her mouth. She flung back the covers and padded barefoot across the wooden floorboards to the bathroom. Swilling peppermint mouthwash around her mouth, she gazed at her reflection in the mirror. It was not exactly a pretty picture. Her skin was pale and glistening. Her short brown hair was a mass of wild curls sticking in all directions and her eyes still held a look of panic from her dream. As she spat out the mouthwash into the round glass sink, the green liquid was tinged with blood. Sticking out her tongue, she could see that it was bleeding. After a few more swills of mouthwash, the bleeding appeared to have stopped and the metallic taste had all but gone. Splashing cold water on her face and running damp fingers through her hair to calm down the curls helped to shake off the remnants of the nightmare. There was no way on earth that she could get back to sleep so, grabbing her thick towelling bath robe from the hook behind the door, she walked back into the bedroom and turned on the bedside lamp. Annie could not help but smile. Bonnie had not taken long to assume the position of owner of the bed during her time in the bathroom. Tying the belt of her dressing gown loosely around her waist, she whistled at her faithful companion. "Come on Bonnie, you know the rules. Floor for you, comfy bed for me!"

Owner and dog walked through the long hallway into the open-plan kitchen and living room. Turning on lights as she walked helped to ease the tension that Annie was still feeling. This had to have been one of the worst nightmares that she had experienced in a long time. The only trouble for Annie was the gnawing fact that she knew deep down that this had been no nightmare. Her years of being a psychic medium had seen her experience 'happenings' from the other side more times than she cared to remember. What she needed to work out was if this particular scenario was something that was about to happen or had already occurred. Either way, this was not what she would call one of her 'good' experiences.

"How about a drink for us both Bonnie?"

After filling up the dog bowl with fresh water, Annie poured some milk into her Dirty Dancing mug and set the timer on the microwave for two minutes. As she watched the mug, complete with its dancing partners, take its slow spin, she tried to take herself back to what it was that had made her wake from the nightmare. This had been the third time in as many weeks where it had been the same dream and it would always end abruptly. Just at the point where she would see the ring and attempt to turn around.

The ding of the microwave brought her back to the present. She reached into the overhead cupboard and pulled out a bottle of Captain Morgan's rum.

"I think we should have a bit of the Captain's 'medicine' tonight eh Bonnie?"

Annie carefully carried her mug across to the office area of her open-plan living room and to what was her favourite part of the house. The floor-to-ceiling picture windows gave her the best living picture that she could ever ask for. Unspoilt views of the ocean complete with the amazing colours and moods that it had to offer. Her desk was made of thick old planks of wood that a good friend had built for her. It was not quite driftwood but he had worked hard to give it the appearance that it had which Annie had been over the moon about. Bonnie had already positioned herself under the desk so, as Annie sat down, she gently nudged her canine friend with her feet, so that she could stick them under Bonnie's more than ample torso, a familiar position for owner and dog and one that came naturally.

Waiting for her Mac to boot up, Annie sat back and gazed out of the window. It was a full moon tonight so the sea had that wonderful artificially lit quality about it that made it both mesmerising and inspirational. The air outside was still, so all that could be heard was the dull thud of the sea as the tide came in. Her reflection stared back at her. Not so mad-eyed and wild haired now, however the paleness of her skin was almost the same as the moon. She was exhausted and the thin pale face looking back at her did nothing to boost her spirits.

The freesias in the vase on her desk were in full bloom and their heady scent always lifted Annie's spirits. She glanced at the photo positioned just beside the vase. Her best friend Lisa smiled back at her looking so beautiful and happy on the arm of her husband Dan. They had been together since they were teenagers and were still as deeply in love now as they were then. Annie had always envied the fact that two people could still feel as strongly for each other after all these years. Her own marriage had been very short and very bitter in comparison and although Lisa still occasionally tried to pair her up with men from Dan's work, Annie resisted it at all costs. For now it was Bonnie and her. She could give out as much love as she wanted and not fear it being rejected by her canine friend.

Taking a sip of her warm milk, Annie felt the rum warm her insides. "The Captain does it again Bonnie". As if in response, Bonnie's tail gave a dull thwack on the floor. Annie opened up the existing file on the computer labelled 'Rope Dream' and started to type in as much as she could remember from tonight's episode. It had become second nature to document her dreams while they were still fresh in her mind. In this way she could build up

a picture of the events, and although none of it was

making any sense just yet, it all helped in her attempt to

piece the jigsaw puzzle of her dream together. She just

hoped that it would make sense soon, as this had been the

first time that she had ever felt physically and mentally

threatened.

Chapter 2

Bonnie's barking woke Annie up. She glanced across at the clock, 7am, and groaned. Annie had not got back to bed until 4am so her body was reluctant to go anywhere soon. Bonnie however was insistent and continued with her barking, which was her way of saying, "Feed me, walk me or else". Annie flung on some jog pants and a sweat top. "Come on then Bonnie, exercise first, food second!"

The day was bright and calm and both owner and dog benefited from the slow, steady jog through the woodland paths. There had been a heavy frost overnight, which had left the ground hard but not too slippy underfoot which was a blessing, as Annie did not relish slipping on her backside while trying to keep up with Bonnie. By the time they arrived back at the house, Annie was feeling more like her old self. Bonnie headed straight for her bowl while Annie made a beeline for the shower.

Washed and feeling almost human again, Annie checked through her post and emails. There was nothing requiring immediate attention and casting a quick glance at her watch warned her that she was running late yet again. She had to drop off Bonnie at Lisa's before heading to the flower shop.

"Come on Bonnie, we need to get going or Lisa will give us both a piece of her mind." Just as she was about to shut the front door, the image of a young man's face appeared. It was blurred but she could tell that he had dark wavy hair and looked happy. The smell of last night came through at the same time, then as quickly as both vision and smell had appeared, they went. Another piece for the puzzle thought Annie and headed to the car where Bonnie was patiently waiting to be let in.

"Morning good-looking, you're looking hot to trot today. You don't look too bad yourself Annie!" Dan chuckled at his own joke while Bonnie made straight for Lisa. Annie gave Dan a thump on his arm.

"One day you will regret these jokes Dan," laughed Lisa.

"Annie will put all your nude baby photos on Facebook

and then you'll be sorry!" Dan pulled a face at them both before heading off to the kitchen to make coffee for them all.

"So how's the patient today?" Annie asked the retreating back of Dan as she followed him through to the kitchen and out of earshot of Lisa.

"She had a really good sleep last night and seems to be relatively pain free today, so I think today may be one of our 'good days'. Fingers crossed."

"What about you Dan, how are you holding up? You're looking tired, plus we haven't talked about the arrangements yet and I know Lisa is going to nag us both soon."

"I can't talk about it yet Annie, I know we need to but just give me a few more weeks. Just let's get Christmas over with first and then start. Okay?"

Annie walked over, stretched up on her toes and gave him a hug. He was such a big strong man who had all the time and love in the world for everyone. To see him struggle with his emotions like this made her heart pull in a million directions. Her loyalty to her best friend and to Dan was being pushed to its limits. She knew that Lisa felt strongly about getting her funeral arrangements finalised soon before she became too weak but Dan was not yet ready to admit that the love of his life only had a short time left to live.

"You have two more weeks Dan and then we need to do what we promised."

Lisa and Bonnie were laid out on the large sofa in front of a roaring fire.

"Thank goodness this sofa is so large Annie, I'm sure your dog is getting even bigger."

Lisa looked flushed from the fire but Annie was more concerned that this was the start of another raging fever. She made a mental note to come back at lunchtime to check.

"Have you remembered that you need to do the Bells' wedding bouquet today?"

Annie nodded while trying to sip coffee and find a space on the sofa to sit close to her friend. "Yep freesias and white roses. Took a bit of persuading as they had all sorts of weird and wonderful colours selected but it would have looked too fussy. They're first on my list when I get to the shop."

Lisa owned the one and only flower shop in the village and it was always busy. Annie put this down more to Lisa's knack with the customers and her ability to make each one feel special, regardless of whether they were buying a single rose or a whole bouquet. Since Lisa's relapse with cancer, Annie had taken over running the shop full-time. Her people skills were perhaps not quite as good as Lisa's. This was partly due to the fact that she would unconsciously pick up feelings from the customers. Some good, some not so good. Lisa always joked that Annie used her psychic 'lie detector' abilities to assess people and therefore avoid the less than honest. In its simplest form, it was her gut-instinct that would sound off the initial warning bells but again her psychic and clairvoyant abilities also helped her. Unfortunately, the same could not be said for her short-lived marriage but then again love, or should that be lust, can get in the way of even the most sensible of people.

"Earth to Annie, come in Annie. Where were you?"

"Sorry, just thinking about love, life and cheating husbands."

"Well, we're all allowed one mistake in life. You've made yours, so now it's time to look for Mr Right."

Annie threw a look at her friend, "I've told you before, it's me and Bonnie from now on. Much less complicated and we have our own routine now. A man would just get in the way."

It was Lisa's turn to pull a face. It was high time her friend found someone who would give her everything that she and Dan had. Annie's husband Ben had been a nasty piece of work and had made Annie's life a living nightmare. The bruises that Annie used to wear told the story of a truly miserable period in her life which thankfully had been stopped quickly. The strength and courage that Annie had shown during that time had amazed both Lisa and Dan. Their concern over their closest friend had been all-consuming and they were both worried about just how much of a beating Annie would take before she said, "no more". Luckily, Annie had realised that this was not the way to live. On one of the frequent occasions when Ben had been working away from home, Annie changed all the locks and took out a restraining order. Months of bitter legal proccedings resulted in divorce and Ben emigrating to America with his new girlfriend. It had left Annie suspicious of all men and reluctant to let anyone close again.

"I'll pop in at lunchtime, to check on you both. Do you want me to bring anything back? What about your medication, are you due some before I go?"

"I'm fine. Dan topped me up half an hour ago so no need to worry. There's no need to come back at lunchtime Bonnie and I will be fine."

"I'm sure Bonnie will, but I don't know about you. You're looking very flushed today."

"It's just the fire. I promise that if I feel unwell I will call either you or Dan. Now those flowers aren't going to make themselves into a stunning wedding bouquet, so get off with you and let Bonnie and I have some rest and relaxation!"

"Okay boss, just behave and chuck Bonnie off if she gets too heavy for you."

Bonnie lifted her head as if to say, "Try it."

Chapter Three

The shop was freezing, however this was by design rather than a fault with the heating. Lisa always liked the shop to be kept cool. In this way, the flowers could remain fresh for as long as possible. Annie would personally have preferred it to be at least a couple of degrees warmer. The only upside to the cold temperature was the fact that the eucalyptus and rosemary delivered yesterday gave the air that special Christmas scent and she could not resist rubbing the eucalyptus leaves between her fingers as she passed them.

Lost in a world of white roses, freesias and a particularly tricky bit of wiring. Annie did not hear the door-chime give off its pleasing tinkling sound. It was not until she heard a gruff cough that she looked up.

"Hello Sidney. Have you been stood there long?"

"Long enough to take in the delights of the vision in front of me."

Annie smiled. Sidney was at least eighty-two years old and still surprisingly sprightly on his feet. Every week he would come in and buy half a dozen yellow roses to place on his wife's grave. Ruby had sadly passed away three months ago but Sidney seemed to be coping with it amazingly well. The only thing that puzzled Annie was the fact that she knew Ruby hated yellow roses, so why did he keep buying them? It was high time she broached the subject.

"Sidney, why don't you buy some of these beautiful lilies today? I could put them together with a bit of eucalyptus and asparagus fern. It would be a lovely Christmas treat for Ruby." She made a move to pick up three stems from the aluminium bucket by her feet but was stopped in her tracks.

"No, Annie. Yellow roses as usual please. That's what my Ruby deserves."

Annie looked up and could see just the faintest of shimmers to the left of Sidney. At exactly the same time she felt that familiar pull in her gut. Something was amiss here but she could not work out what it was and she was not sure that he would appreciate her asking. For a split second she could have sworn she heard Ruby's voice and the words, '*I'm sorry.*' Wrapping the roses up in white paper, Annie took a sneaky look across at Sidney to see if she could still see the shimmer beside him. She felt sure that this was the presence of Ruby but wanted to take her time and if possible, tune into what was going on.

"Are you eyeing me up young lady?"

Annie laughed, "Sorry Sidney. I just thought that you were looking extra dapper today and if I was just two years older then I may have asked you out on a date."

Sidney chuckled, "You'll have to get in the queue Annie."

As he left the shop clutching his roses, Annie could still see the shimmering form following him. There was obviously a story to tell here but she was going to have to wait a while before she found out what it was.

Half an hour later, the bouquet was finished and boxed up ready to be delivered. Taking the van keys off the hook, Annie was about to close up the shop when suddenly the image of the young man she had seen earlier appeared. This time she could see exactly what he was wearing. A red sweat top with lettering along the front, as well as a pair of faded blue jeans, with a rip in the knee. A pair of blue trainers with a yellow stripe across the toes completed the ensemble. Then it was gone. She quickly ripped a sheet of paper from the memo pad and jotted down what she had seen along with the name of Kevin.

"Now where on earth did that come from?"

"Talking to yourself Annie? You do know that it is regarded as the first sign of madness?"

Annie had been so distracted with her 'vision' that she had not heard Richard come into the shop. He had to be one of the most naturally handsome men she had ever met. He never made an effort as far as his appearance was concerned but he always looked good.

"Long time no see Richard. How are things?" Annie quickly glanced in the shop window to check her reflection. She may have been put off men for life but this did not mean that she did not want to look presentable in front of someone like him. The mad eyed look was long gone thank goodness but her hair looked as though she had been dragged through a bush backwards.

"Fine thanks Annie. Just come up to see Mum and Dad for the Christmas break and then I'm back off to London." Without realising, Annie had already started to put together a small posy of white lilies and roses as well as some eucalyptus and white freesia.

"Are you doing that for me? How did you know what I was going to ask for Annie?"

Annie looked down at the ensemble. She could hardly say, 'Oh well, I was using my psychic powers...' so instead opted for a safer choice of excuse.

"They just look so good together at this time of year that I thought you would like them for your mum."

Richard smiled, "Well thanks Annie, it's much appreciated. Are you spending Christmas with Lisa and Dan?"

Annie nodded as she handed over the arrangement.

"Do you think Lisa is up for a visit? I'd love to see them both before I go back to London and I won't be back up in Dornoch for another six months so......." He left the sentence unfinished but they both knew that what he had been about to say was that he did not know if Lisa would still be alive in another six months. He looked down at his feet.

"Sorry Annie, it's just so difficult to know what to say in a situation like this."

Without thinking she reached forward and gently stroked his arm, "It's okay Richard. We are all just taking one day at a time and yes she would love to see you. I think Dan could probably do with another man in the house for a couple of hours as he has me, Lisa and Bonnie nagging him almost all the time. Although I think he secretly enjoys it!"

After he left the shop, Annie could not help but wonder what it would be like to be in a relationship again. Her time with Ben had been so painful. He had been the love of her life, or so she thought. While they had dated he had been the epitome of the perfect gentleman. Always attentive and caring. It had only been once they had married that everything had changed. The first signs had been evident while on honeymoon, but Annie had tried to ignore them. It was not until they had arrived home that she fully became aware of the other side of Ben. His temper and the use of his fists came into their own and Annie had always wondered why she had not seen the signs earlier. It still confused her and made her so cautious now. Just every now and then she would love to have the arms of someone around her, who could give her what she needed. Especially now with all that was going on with Lisa.

"You're just feeling sorry for yourself, don't let your guard down lady," Annie muttered as she closed up the shop to make her deliveries. It did not stop her looking down the street at Richard's departing figure.

Chapter Four

He did not know why he felt as if he was being watched, but it was definitely making him feel nervous. Taking another sip from his pint of beer, he tried to look interested in the newspaper in front of him. Looking up, he could see that there were two middle-aged men staring at him. He quickly glanced back down at his paper. Why did he feel so nervous? He was on a break, enjoying a quiet pint in a local pub, soaking up the local atmosphere, which until ten minutes ago had been relaxed and amiable. Then he had started to feel uneasy and now he could see that these two men were staring at him and talking quite animatedly to each other.

As he stood up to go, one of the men also stood up and casually walked towards him.

"Business or pleasure?"

"I'm sorry?"

"Well, it's an odd time of the year to be on the island. It's not exactly warm here at this time of the year."

"It's a bit of both actually. I'm on the mainland for business but have a few days off to take in the scenery." Kevin already felt as if he had said too much but the man had, in effect, blocked his way out of the bar.

"Well, enjoy your time here on the island." He put out his hand as if to shake and Kevin could not help but notice the odd pattern of the ring he wore on his finger.

"I will, thanks." With a brief shake of his hand, Kevin made a quick getaway to his rental car parked out front. As he drove away, he glanced in his rearview mirror and could see the man standing in the middle of the road, watching the car depart.

Chapter Five

"You'll never guess who called me this afternoon to ask if they could visit."

"Richard."

"How the hell did you know that?"

"Well, I could say that I used my psychic skills but that would be lying. He came into the shop earlier today to buy some flowers for his mum. We got talking and he asked if you were up for a visit."

"So what does he look like these days? Still got that casual untamed look about him?"

Annie knew that Lisa was trying to slowly reel her in to saying that he was looking good but she would not take the bait. "About the same really, can't say I noticed. I was about to leave with the wedding order."

Lisa did not look convinced but just at that point Bonnie had shifted her weight across her legs and it was starting to hurt. "Annie, get your great lump of a dog off me please. I would like to still be able to walk!"

With a quick shove, Bonnie was unceremoniously ejected off the sofa. Throwing a rather hurt look at the girls, she flopped down in front of the fire and promptly went back to sleep.

"You spoil that dog, it's about time you moved your attention to good looking young men."

Annie pretended not to hear. "What time is Dan getting back tonight?"

"In about an hour. He went in late as he had a few things to sort out here first. Are you staying for dinner tonight?"

Annie was tempted but she wanted to get back and type up her notes that she had made while in the shop. She spent the next few minutes outlining her dream and her latest vision to Lisa.

"So do you think it has already happened then?"

"I really don't know. That's what I'm trying to work out at the moment. I'm just hoping that my next dream will give me a little bit more of the picture."

Lisa's face showed the concern she felt for her friend.

"Don't let this get to you Annie. You're looking really tired and I know what you're like once you get your teeth into something."

"I'm fine, don't worry about it. Anyway I'm staying over here tomorrow night so you and Dan can keep an eye on me then." Lisa still looked concerned but she was in no position to lecture Annie. Before her illness, if Annie had experienced any psychic visions like this then she had been the first to encourage Annie to find out more and they would go off on what Dan often termed 'wild goose chases'. He had been made to eat his words on more than one occasion however. In the past couple of years, Annie had helped several individuals who had lost family members in what could only be termed as mysterious circumstances. The last one being a young teenage girl who had run away from home due to a fight with her parents. Annie had read about it in the local paper and had immediately picked up, from the picture, information about the girl that could only be known by her parents. After a large amount of persuading by Lisa, Annie had approached the parents with her information and luckily they had been receptive. There had been times in the past when she had had doors slammed in her face or worse, been called a witch.

"Come on Bonnie, home time."

"Oh Annie, did I say that I had arranged for Richard to come round tomorrow night for a meal with us?"

Annie threw her friend a withering look. "You never stop trying do you? It won't work."

"It's my dying wish to see you with someone Annie. You wouldn't want to go against a dying woman's wish would you?"

"Not funny! Go and meddle elsewhere."

Lisa chuckled as Annie and Bonnie left. Annie may have the psychic powers but she had the matchmaking skills and she was determined to have her best friend settled with someone before she died, even though she knew that Annie was going to be a tough nut to crack on this one.

Chapter Six

Annie opened up the file on her mac, to update it with her latest 'visions'. The list was not exactly lengthy and she had a horrible feeling that she was missing something blatantly obvious. So far, her list comprised of the following short statements:-

Night-time

Fear/panic

Smell and sound of the sea

Rope – coarse and thick

Slimy, dark rocks

Man – strong arms

Ring finger – can't see the ring but I know it means something

Kevin – mid to late 20's?

Dark curly hair

Red sweat-top with lettering, blue faded jeans, blue trainers with yellow stripe

Why do I think that it is abroad?

She leant back in her chair, gazing out at the early

evening view. It had been another surprisingly mild day considering that they were in the Highlands of Scotland and there were only a few days left until Christmas. Perhaps global warming was coming as far up as Dornoch after all, she mused.

As she drank her coffee and warmed her feet underneath Bonnie's rump, she still could not believe that Lisa was trying to set her up with someone even at Christmas. It really was as if she was determined to see her settled with someone before she died. There was no way that Annie was going to give in to emotional blackmail, even if it was her best friend's desire. It was hard enough knowing that she had such a short time left with the only person that she trusted implicitly. Annie's parents had passed away several years ago. Thankfully they had not suffered the anguish of seeing their much-loved daughter go through a messy, painful marriage and divorce. She had been an only child so she was quite literally on her own. Lisa and Dan were her only family now, which made it seem even unfair that their time together would now be so short.

Bonnie lifted her head and gazed at Annie, almost as if she knew that her owner needed some love.

"Come on Bonnie, dinner time."

This was the type of conversation that Bonnie liked. Owner and dog padded across to the kitchen area. Bonnie to her bowl looking up expectantly at Annie. Once dog food had been dutifully poured into the bowl and Bonnie was happily munching away, Annie turned her attention to what she could cook for herself. There was a Jamie Oliver recipe that she had wanted to try for ages. This was one thing that Annie had always been insistent upon, even though she was living on her own. She would not let herself fall into the ready meal brigade, which could be so easy to do. Annie and Lisa had both spent time on cookery night school courses, as they loved to experiment and they were always trying out new recipes and exchanging hints and tips. Tonight however she wanted something quick and simple. After steaming some spinach, she added in some nutmeg and seasoning then poured in some mascarpone cheese and double cream.

"Think I'll need to run again tomorrow Bonnie!" She added in the pasta that she had already cooked and mixed it all round while at the same time letting her mind wander. Richard had looked really good today. He had that strong silent look about him that she was always attracted to but he also seemed to be incredibly considerate to those around him, which was unusual these days. Or at least for Annie it was. The ringing of her mobile brought her back to reality.

"What are you doing?"

"Well, Jamie and I are getting up close and personal with some spinach and mascarpone. What about you?"

"I was just wondering about the seating arrangements for tomorrow night. Should it be girl, available boy, ill friend and long-suffering husband, or would you prefer a table for two?"

"Don't pull the ill friend one on me lady! I'm off men for life you know that."

"Me think the lady does protest too much but I'll let you off as you are bringing the dessert!"

"So, did you ring just to tease or was there a purpose to this call?"

"It was just to say why don't you and Bonnie stay over for the next few nights. We both know that this will be our last Christmas together. Plus you know I don't like you being in that big old house on your own."

Lisa had always been very upfront about her illness and had accepted that there was not going to be a happy ever after ending to it. Her approach was typical Lisa: practical and to the point but Annie was still finding it hard to accept.

"Bonnie and I would love to stay. I do hope that this invite is being extended just to us and not to any other guests."

"Now there's an idea. Is this your way of asking me to give him a call?"

They both laughed and after a few more minutes of conversation regarding an order for the shop, Annie hung up the phone. Carefully carrying her plate across to the dining table she took in the sunset that was now filling the whole of her picture window. The sky had that brilliant orange hue that then seems to transform into a multitude of pinks. The sea was a wonderful mix of lavender shades and in the far distance she could see the flicker of streetlights along the Black Isle headland. It was at moments like these that she realised just how lucky she was. She may be divorced and, to all intents and purposes an orphan, but her parents had left her a large amount of money in their will. The house had been her one luxury purchase, otherwise she was frugal, or 'tight' as Lisa would sometimes say. The minute she had walked into this house and taken in the fantastic floor to ceiling picture windows, which ran from one end of the room to the other she was sold. Her short marriage had been spent in this house but Annie had no qualms about staying here. This was and always had been her home and the only concession to Ben's short time spent here had been when she had to change the locks.

As Annie washed up the dinner dishes, she let her mind wander back to the mysterious Kevin. The feelings she had experienced over the past few days were much stronger than she was used to and she felt sure that this was an incident that had yet to occur. But how to stop it? What on earth could she do from here? At this point she did not even know if he was in the same country as her. Just as the thought came into her head, she suddenly heard the words *'azure window'*. She quickly turned but could see no one in the room, either human or spirit.

Bonnie had lifted her head though, which was always a

sign that she was picking up on some spiritual activity

and Annie followed the dog's gaze. Out of the corner of

her eye she was sure that she could see the faint outline of

a middle-aged woman. Annie stepped forward, squinting

as she moved to see if she could make the 'figure' out any

clearer. As she walked forward the smell of cigars came

wafting across. Slightly odd considering the spectre in

front of her was a woman, from what she could see.

"Are you warning me about Kevin?"

Again the waft of cigar smoke came across the room, but

the figure itself was not moving.

"What do you want me to do?"

As soon as she had asked the question, Annie felt herself

become very light-headed. At the same time a number of

images flashed in front of her. Some she could make out

quite clearly however others just seemed like meaningless

shapes. Then they were gone.

Annie semi-sprinted, semi-slid across the floor to her desk

as she needed to write down everything she could

remember. Luckily the file was still open where she had left it. She added in the new information:-

Azure window

White chapel

Blue garage door

Red tractor

Cigar smoke – female spirit

Danger – Keep Out

Annie shook her head. None of it made sense when she looked at it in black and white but at least she was keeping a log. Out of curiosity, she googled 'azure window'. The search engine returned a number of results which all seemed to link back to the same place. A small island named Gozo, which was close to Malta. "Never heard of it, have you Bonnie?" Bonnie had resumed her sprawled out position under the desk, apparently none the worse for her earlier spiritual experience. Annie shut down the computer making a mental note to dig out some more information about Gozo. Perhaps Lisa would know something about the island. She wrote down on a yellow sticky note pad by her keyboard 'Gozo – Lisa' and stuck it on her screen to

remind her in the morning.

Chapter Seven

She woke up again at exactly the same place in the dream. Her body soaked in sweat and her heart racing, only this time there was one extra nugget of information. The ring had an engraving of a crown on it and in the centre of the crown was a very small green stone. She leant over and jotted it down on the pad she had placed on her bedside table, just in case she had another dream. She lay back in the bed and drew the covers up over her eyes as if that would stop it coming back.

Bonnie jumped up onto the bed and lay down by Annie's feet and for once, Annie did not tell her to get off, as the feeling of comfort was reassuring. As she drifted back to sleep the faint smell of cigar smoke was back in the room. It felt as if she was being protected and guided rather than warned off, so she let herself drift back into sleep with Bonnie and her female, cigar smoking spirit visitor keeping a watchful eye over her.

Chapter Eight

Kevin looked out of his hotel window. He was sure he recognised the car parked across from the hotel but he could not be sure. The gnawing feeling in the pit of his stomach was still there. He could not shake off the feeling that he was being watched. The feeling had been with him ever since his visit to the bar earlier that day, from which he had made a hasty exit.

The laptop gave a chirrup sound indicating an incoming message. He glanced out the window one last time before walking over to his computer. It was an email from his manager back at the UK Head Office. The sales meeting that Kevin had attended in Malta a couple of days before had gone very well. The company had asked if he could possibly go back into their offices, before he left for England, so that they could discuss figures in detail. Reading between the lines, his boss was indicating that it would be beneficial for Kevin if he delayed his flight for a day so that he could build up relations with these potential new clients. He sent a brief message back confirming that yes; he would stay over, and hit the send button.

That was the easy bit. He now had to ring his wife Karen to break the news. She was not going to be happy. However if he managed to finalise this deal, then his bonus would be just what they needed to keep them financially afloat, while Karen took time off work to look after their first child, which was due in April.

Sitting at the hotel bar, Kevin reflected on the conversation that he had just had with Karen. You could have cut the air with a knife. To say that she had been angry must have been the understatement of the year. Tears and angry words had ensued with both of them saying things that Kevin knew he would be made to regret for weeks if not years to come. All he was asking for was a couple more days. He would still be back in time for Christmas Day, although he was probably going to have to do the majority of his Christmas shopping at the Duty Free shops! He sighed and took another long sip of his cold beer. He loved Karen but at times he did wonder what path their future would take. The past couple of years had been incredibly hard for them both. His job had meant that he would spend weeks away from home carrying out deals in other countries. This in turn had resulted in Karen having a fling with a work colleague. He had only found out about it six months ago and she had promised faithfully that it was all over, but there was a nagging feeling in the pit of his stomach that she had not been telling the truth.

They had agreed to give the marriage another go, and a few weeks after a romantic and slightly drunken evening, Karen had found that she was pregnant. Both of them were shocked but pleased at the same time. Would their marriage be strong enough to handle a third person in their relationship, especially when it was still in a fragile state? Only time would tell but Kevin knew he had not done himself any favours by delaying his trip home.

Chapter Nine

Annie woke up to Bonnie's face on the pillow beside her. So much for the ground rules. She did have to admit to herself that she had not exactly discouraged Bonnie from joining her on the bed last night, after yet another bad dream. She gave the dog a shove, which was enough of a signal for her to realise that her time of sleeping comfort was over and she had better get off quick!

As she stripped off the bed sheets, Annie could not help but dwell on how important this Christmas was going to be. She had promised herself that she would not cry and that she would be strong for Dan however she was finding that this was easier said than done. Lisa's mum had died of cervical cancer ten years ago and it had been a terrible thing to watch. She had gone from being a strong, outgoing woman who did everything for herself to what Lisa and Annie felt had been an empty shell in a matter of six months. It had been a harrowing experience for all concerned and Annie did not want her friend to suffer as Lisa's mum had done. Pain relief had moved on since then but Annie could still remember the screams that she could hear from Lisa's mum when it had become unbearable.

'Please god don't let Lisa suffer that way. Make it quick and painless please,' thought Annie.

The ring of the front doorbell made her jump a mile. She dumped the sheets at the foot of the bed and headed for the front door, however Bonnie had the same idea. The pair of them bowled into one another, causing Annie to fall flat on her back, as the wooden floor was too slippy to keep her balance.

"Bloody hell Bonnie, watch what you are doing!"

By now, Bonnie was at the door, tail thumping away as it was unusual for anyone to come visiting. As the doorbell rang again, Annie carefully got up from the floor. No bones broken but maybe she should take Lisa's advice and cut down on the amount she fed Bonnie. That had been one hell of a knock down!

"Richard, what a surprise!" and she meant it. She knew she would not exactly be looking her ravishing best and after her tenpin bowling experience with Bonnie, she was feeling winded and a dull ache was making itself known from her hip. What made it worse was that he was holding a huge bunch of flowers in front of him and looked like something straight out of a television commercial.

"Have I come at a bad time?"

"No, it's fine. Come in. Bonnie and I were not expecting visitors so you have caught us on the hop so to speak," she moved back and opened the door wider to let him in. As he walked past, she caught the whiff of Aramis. Always a soft spot with her. She shook her head, this had to be Lisa's doing.

"Is everything alright? I thought I heard a bang just before you came to the door?"

Annie threw Bonnie a glower; "Yep, Bonnie and I had a collision on the way to the door. Unfortunately I came off worse than her. I'm pretty sure that I will have a bruised backside before the day is out." Richard chuckled as they carried on walking into her lounge.

"So, what brings you out here Richard? We're a little off the beaten track to be just passing."

"Well, I hope you don't mind.......Lisa said that she usually comes with you to your mum and dad's graves today. We were talking about it on the phone yesterday. She asked me if I would mind standing in for her this year, what with her being......." he tailed off, slightly embarrassed.

"Did she now? It's lovely of you to have agreed but I'm more than happy to go on my own. I apologise if Lisa bullied you, she can be quite determined when she wants."

"Yes, I never could say no to her you know. She has a certain way about her, which makes everyone just want to please her. Quite a gift really."

"Mmmm," Annie raised an eyebrow. She had forgotten that before Dan and Lisa had hooked up, Richard had quite a crush on her. "Where are my manners? Come and sit down and I'll put the kettle on. It would be good to catch up on all your latest news from the big city. We don't get much action around here you know."

Richard looked slightly unsure what he should do with the flowers in his hands. Annie quickly took them off him.

"I'll pop these in some water for now, just to keep them

fresh. By the way where did you get these from? They have a familiar style to them that I would usually put down to Lisa."

It was Richard's turn to raise an eyebrow, "Guilty as charged. She made Dan open up the shop early this morning with a list of exactly what she wanted."

Annie shook her head. Lisa was always putting other people before her. It must have taken quite a bit out of her. Perhaps she should cancel tonight's meal. As if reading her mind Richard turned from looking out of the picture windows.

"Do not even think about cancelling tonight! I was given strict instructions to make sure that you don't bale out on her," he casually strolled over to where she was standing. "Annie, you look exhausted. This is taking its toll on both you and Dan. Why not let me help a bit while I'm here?"

This threw Annie. She had not expected an offer of help from someone that she only saw perhaps three times a year, but then again she knew that he kept in regular contact with Dan.

"Well, thanks for the flattering comment. I suppose it does no harm to humour Lisa while you are here for the holidays. Dan would appreciate someone to talk to as well."

"Good. That settles it then. How about that coffee and then we could walk over to the cemetery. That is, if it's okay with you?"

Annie nodded, "That would be lovely, thanks Richard."

Chapter Ten

Karen gently rubbed her tummy, trying to visualise the baby growing inside her. It was a big risk to take, having a baby after all that had happened. She knew that Kevin was still hurting from her affair but that was all over with now. In some ways it had been her way of hitting out at him. He was never home. Always away on deals.

A small elbow raised itself from under her belly; she could not help but smile. Such a wonderful thing to witness, so special, which was why she had reacted badly to Kevin's phone call. He was missing something wonderful just to secure another deal. Was it really worth it? As usual she had hit out verbally at him and now regretted it. She picked up the phone and dialled his number for the third time that day. Irritation started to rise when it went straight to voicemail again.

"Call me," and with that she hung up. It was unlike Kevin not to answer. He must have thought that after their last conversation that she was about to give him some more verbal abuse. She stroked her tummy again; "We just want him home don't we?"

Chapter Eleven

The frost crunched under their feet as they headed up the hill to the cemetery. Ironically, Annie had always loved the walk to her parents' graves. The winding path took you past some wonderful views of the Dornoch Firth and in the summer the smell of the wild honeysuckle was captivating.

Today however was a typical winter's day in Dornoch. It was cold enough to make your lips numb and your fingertips ache, which was why she had ensured that she put on a pair of thick woollen gloves as well as a hat and scarf. Richard was equally attired. They kept the pace brisk in an effort to keep warm. Bonnie loped ahead; occasionally stopping to look back at Annie and Richard as if to say, "Hurry up".

Annie had been surprised at how easy Richard was to talk to. He was a good listener and she realised that it was just what she needed at the moment.

As they approached the gravestones of Annie's parents,

Bonnie was already sitting down beside them looking expectantly at Annie, who rummaged in her pocket and brought out a handful of dog biscuits.

"Here you go mutt."

Bonnie wagged her tail and settled down with her small prize of biscuits.

"Don't you think you should ration her? She is quite a large dog, more like a small horse really," joked Richard.

"How can you possibly deny those eyes? I bet you would be just the same with her if she was yours."

Richard laughed, "Well you certainly can't deny that she's being looked after. Do you want some time on your own? I can go for a walk and come back when you're ready."

Annie shook her head, "It's fine, I just like to come up here before Christmas to put some flowers down. I won't get all mushy, I promise you."

He gave her a wry grin, "I think Lisa would like nothing better than for you to get all teary and fall into my arms!"

Annie gave an involuntary gasp, she had not realised that Richard had cottoned on to Lisa's ploy but what was even more embarrassing for Annie was how enticing the thought was!

"It's okay Annie. I'm not angry with Lisa. I'm actually very flattered that she thinks that I am a suitable beau for her best friend. She is very protective of you, you know. In fact, I'm pretty sure that she carries out a screening process on any would be admirers."

"It does seem to be her ambition to see me hooked up with someone. I just wish she would leave it. It's hard enough knowing that there isn't much time left with her without complicating matters." Annie's voice broke and she quickly turned her back to Richard, in pretence of fussing with the flowers. He very gently put an arm around her shoulders.

"Annie, you can only handle so much on your own. I want to help you all, as much as I can. I just don't know how you and Dan keep so upbeat. I think if I was in Dan's shoes I would be in a much darker place and probably no help to Lisa at all."

Although she felt awkward having his arm around her shoulders, it also felt strangely nice to have someone to lean on, just a little bit. Despite feeling upset, she giggled.

Richard looked down at her.

"Care to share the joke?"

"She would be dancing around if she could see us now."

"Well, we could always play along with her a bit to keep her happy if you want," and with that he released his arm from her shoulders. Suddenly Annie wanted that protective arm back around her. It had felt good, warm. She shook her head as if to shake off any silly thoughts about love and romance. Richard carried on looking at her with a slightly bemused look on his face.

"Any particular reason for the head shaking or is it something you do when you come up here?" His eyes had a cheeky glint to them as he looked down at Annie, making him seem even more attractive to her.

"Sorry, just having a conversation in my head about being sensible. I'm sworn off men now or hasn't Lisa told you that bit?"

"Dan told me about what happened with Ben but I never really knew if I should say anything. I'm really sorry that you went through such a bad time Annie. Just remember we're not all like that. In fact, us guys can get just as hurt as you females."

Something in his tone made Annie look up at him and although she knew that she shouldn't, she decided to see if she could pick up anything psychically from him. Quick flashes of colour as well as a feeling of depression came over her along with the name Lucy. Without thinking she asked, "Who's Lucy?"

He took a step back, looking startled. She realised, as soon as she had said it, that this was stepping over the invisible line that she had with friends. As a rule she did not use any of her clairvoyant and psychic abilities with friends unless asked. To make matters worse, she didn't think that he knew anything about her so-called talent. It was not something that she openly talked about. This was going to be awkward.

"Where did you hear that name from Annie? I've never mentioned her to anyone here, not even my parents." He was looking more puzzled than angry which was a relief to Annie but she wasn't quite sure how to proceed. Should she admit to what she could do and scare off someone who had just offered her and Dan a helping hand in what was a difficult time for them both, or should she just keep her trap shut?

"Hang on a minute. You started putting flowers together for me the other day before I had even asked."

Annie smiled, "Well, you were in a flower shop so I hardly thought that you had come in for a tin of beans."

A small smile played on his lips, which was a relief to Annie but she was still concerned as to what his reaction was going to be.

"Now I come to think about it, you've always been a bit spooky like that. I remember at school you used to come out with things that just seemed like utter madness but you were always right about them. Do you remember the time when you asked me about my little brother and was he alright? I didn't know until I got home that he had fallen badly when out with mum at the park and broken his arm. Do you remember that?" He was looking at her with a baffled expression on his face but at least he wasn't walking away which Annie had experienced with other men.

"Yep, I'm just a bit weird, that's all."

"Well, I know that, but this is something more! I can tell by your face that you are holding back on something. Come on, share the secret."

Just at that moment Bonnie let out a loud bark. They both turned in her direction but nothing was there, or rather there was nothing visible for Richard to see.

"What's up Bonnie?" Richard gently stroked the top of Bonnie's head. By this time Bonnie had assumed the position of laying flat out, nose between paws and only her eyes gave the game away that she was still seeing something. Annie took the opportunity to follow Bonnie's gaze, while Richard was distracted. Sure enough, just ahead of them was the shimmering shape of a person. Annie closed her eyes and took a deep breath, trying to tune out the presence of Richard and to become more receptive to whomever it was that had decided to make an appearance in the middle of a graveyard. She was suddenly transported back to the cliff-top of her dreams and she could smell cigar smoke all around her almost as if it was keeping her protected. Then suddenly, it hit her.

"They've got the wrong person!"

"I beg your pardon?"

Annie's eyes flew open. The presence had gone and all that was left was the faint whiff of cigar smoke. She hadn't realised that she had spoken out loud. How on earth was she going to talk her way out of this? In the past, whenever she had started to explain to other people about her 'special skill' she had found that they had either walked away or laughed at her. It was difficult to judge which approach Richard would take and she really didn't have the energy to try to explain everything.

"Annie, what did you just say?" By now Richard was starting to look concerned but Annie could tell that he wasn't quite sure what to do.

"Sorry Richard. Just thinking out loud about something, that's all."

"Bit of an odd thing to say though. They've got the wrong person. It's more like something you would hear on a cop film. Not the kind of thing you say at a graveyard." He was half laughing as he said it but it was obvious that he was wondering if she was having the start of a breakdown in front of him. Luckily for Annie, her phone rang. He raised an eyebrow at the ringtone. The Dirty Dancing theme tune. Lisa's ringtone. Annie quickly pulled her mobile from her pocket.

"You okay Lisa?"

"Fine, don't panic every time I ring your bloody mobile."

"Alright, message received. So........the purpose of your phone call is?"

"Apparently the alarm is going off at the shop. Dan can't have set it properly when he left there this morning. He's still at the office, could you pop round and check everything is okay?" As Lisa was talking Annie gave Richard the thumbs up sign to let him know that Lisa was fine.

"No problem, I'll get over there now. I'll ring you from the shop just to let you know that I've got there and haven't been beaten to a pulp by a flower robbing thief."

"I'm more worried that you get a mouthful from the residents having to listen to that god awful noise. Sorry Annie. I know that you're at your Mum and Dad's graves." Now wasn't the time for Annie to give her a lecture in regards to her graveside companion. That could wait until later.

Putting the phone back into her pocket, she explained to Richard about the shop alarm.

"I'll come with you, just in case. You never know at this time of year, maybe someone was hoping that there was money in the till." He took her hand which made Annie give him a sharp, questioning look.

"I'm not getting fresh Annie. It's just that the path back down is really slippy so I'd rather have hold of you now in case you go falling. You always were a bit clumsy."

"Alright, but don't start getting any ideas! Come on Bonnie, time to go."

Walking back down the hill, they kept the conversation light and there was no further mention of her earlier outburst although she knew that he was not going to let it go that easily.   For now she was quite enjoying the light conversation and the firm grip of his hand.

Chapter Twelve

Putting the final touches to the Christmas presents gave Annie the time she needed to still her mind before heading off to Lisa's. She had found it difficult keeping herself in check today with Richard. As lovely as it had been to let him hug her at the cemetery, she just did not want to have the additional emotional baggage that letting him into her life may cause. His offer to help both her and Dan while he was here as genuine enough and she was certainly not going to refuse any help. It simply came down to the fact that she did not want anything else. Not just now.

In front of her lay Lisa's gift. In previous years, they would buy each other a mound of presents as if they were still kids, both trying to outdo each other on the tackiest present that they could find. Lisa always seemed to find real gems and Annie smiled remembering the year that Lisa had bought her a mug. It had a picture of an incredibly hunky, well-dressed male on it but as you poured hot water into it, the clothes started to slowly disappear revealing a naked man. Annie had only realised this while drinking coffee out of it for the first time in front of her mum!

She had got her own back the following year with a pair of musical knickers. In fact, she could still remember Dan's face when Lisa had put them on without telling him and when she sat down for Christmas Dinner with his parents, 'Jingle Bells' had started playing.

This year, Annie wanted Lisa to have something that would symbolise their friendship and how much it had meant to her over all these years. She had come across the ideal present quite by chance when out on a delivery a couple of months ago. Nestled in a tiny box was a necklace with a single delicate butterfly made out of rose quartz. As she held it up to the light, it looked so fragile. Just like Lisa is now, she thought. Placing it back carefully in its box, she wrapped it up in soft pink tissue and signed the card 'love, me xx' No other message was necessary.

With a heavy sigh, she packed the rest of the presents into her weekend bag, ready to take to Lisa and Dan's. Walking through the house, she half closed the blinds to give the house that 'lived in' look while she was away and made sure that the timer for the lights was set. Suddenly, the hairs on the back of her neck stood on end. Cigar smoke drifted past her nostrils. She very slowly turned towards the direction that the smell seemed to be coming from. Her gut-instinct told her that this was the same woman who now seemed to be 'popping in' daily. The sense of urgency also seemed to be increasing. In the corner of the hallway there was an air of lightness in what was usually a dark area. Annie's psychic and clairvoyant abilities usually worked around emotions and general feelings of a room rather than seeing full-blown apparitions. Tonight was definitely going to prove to be an exception. As her eyes grew accustomed to the gloom, she could see the form of an elderly lady in front of her. This lady had what could be best termed as a stocky frame and as Annie watched her, she held up her right hand and with her left hand pointed at the missing tip of her index finger. Annie slowly closed her eyes and took a deep breath. She tried to empty her mind of everything, in the hope that this woman could then give her either a message or some more images. The air around her became warm and had an earthy smell. An image of a small outbuilding with a blue painted wooden door and a shiny new padlock appeared in her head, then quickly changed to a large expanse of the clearest blue water that she had ever seen. As she turned her head, she could see steps coming down from a cliff path and ending at a small sandy cove. With her eyes still closed but turning her head as if she was physically looking at her surroundings, she could see a small red and white boat anchored just a small distance ahead of her. No one appeared to be in it and she could just see the letters ANT at the far end. Then, as quickly as it had appeared, it was gone. The cigar smell had dispersed and the corner of the hall had gone dark again.

Annie was feeling more confused than ever. She was being given small pieces of information but they were not giving her a bigger and clearer picture. The danger now was that she would make her own assumptions, which could be way off the mark. On her desk lay a print out of what she had already logged on her computer. She quickly jotted down the rest of the information. Lisa was always good at these puzzles. She had a knack of dragging out of Annie the smallest nuggets of information that were held deep within her subconscious which she had either not clearly seen or registered. Folding it up and placing it carefully in a side pocket of her bag, she whistled to Bonnie who was still laid out prone under Annie's desk. Her outdoor activities had obviously taken their toll.

"Come on Bonnie. Let's get over to Lisa's and make sure she's not up to any more matchmaking mischief." Picking up her bag, she headed out the front door. The tiniest of snowflakes were just starting to make their way down from the whitest of skies. Annie lifted her face skywards, closing her eyes as the flakes landed on her cheeks.

"A white Christmas. Now that would be a lovely last Christmas for us all to spend together. Come on mutt, let's get going."

Chapter Thirteen

Lisa and Dan were stood at opposite ends of the kitchen, putting the final touches to the evening meal. A comfortable silence lay between them as they carried out their tasks. Dan was humming to a song playing on the radio while cutting up some vegetables. Lisa smiled at his tuneless humming and snuck a look at him. He still made her heart skip a beat, even after all this time together. Her one regret was that they had not had the time to have the family that they had always talked about. She realised with hindsight that it had been a blessing now that her cancer had returned, but she could not help but wonder what they would have looked like. It was on days like today when she was feeling good and the pain was being managed that her thoughts would drift to the 'what ifs' but she knew that although she felt well today, it could all change by tomorrow.

Headlights swooped past the kitchen window and Dan glanced up, "Annie's arrived. Now behave missus."

"I don't know what you mean."

He threw her a withering look, "You know exactly what I'm on about! You have got to be the worst liar in the world. If Annie wants a relationship with someone then she'll do it when she is good and ready." He could not help but smile at the innocent expression that Lisa was attempting to pull.

"I'm shocked and stunned. How could you think that I would meddle?"

Dan chuckled, "Never kid a kidder." He wrapped his arms around her and buried his face in her hair, "You smell good enough to eat."

"Thank you kindly," lifting up her face she gently kissed him. "I love you so much Dan, you do know that don't you?"

"Never doubted it for a moment." He kissed the nape of her neck and held her tight. His heart was fit to break. She was so thin and vulnerable now but he knew that she did not want to be treated any differently although it was hard not to.

"Oh for God's sake you two get a room!"

Bonnie padded over towards the cooking smells, while Annie dumped her bag in the hallway. "Is this what you two do when cooking dinner? I'll need a sick bag at this rate."

Lisa threw a tea towel at Annie, "Stop moaning and dry some of these dishes before Richard arrives."

Annie smiled, Lisa was looking the best she had seen her in weeks and Dan had lost some of the tension that seemed to be permanently etched around his eyes. The cancer was taking its toll on them all in some shape or form.

"Mulled wine ladies?"

"Yes please Dan."

"I'll just have water thanks, I'll keep my wine treat until after the meal." Lisa was not supposed to drink alcohol with her medication but she was going to make an exception to the rule tonight. As Dan poured the drinks, the doorbell rang, signalling the arrival of Richard.

"Behave," chorused Dan and Annie.

"Honestly, you two have such a low opinion of me."

"Years of experience Lisa. You may be my best friend but you don't half meddle."

Lisa stuck out her tongue and made her way to the front door. "Richard, it's great to see you again and I must say that you are looking especially handsome tonight. Isn't he Annie?"

Annie rolled her eyes while Dan half choked on his mulled wine.

"Have I just walked into the end of a joke at my expense by any chance?"

"No Richard, it's just this pair of children being silly."

He arched an eyebrow at Annie who winked back at him. When they had stopped off at the flower shop to check out the alarm, they had agreed on a plan if Lisa started to drop unsubtle hints. If Annie winked at Richard then that was his signal to put into action their 'bluffing plan'. So, taking his cue, he casually walked across to Annie and put his arms around her and gave her a kiss full on the lips.

"Hi gorgeous."

"Hi yourself," Annie sneaked a glance at Lisa while struggling to keep a straight face.

"Lisa, close your mouth you're in danger of catching flies," joked Dan.

Richard had already moved across to where Dan was stood and was in the process of opening a bottle of beer. The boys were both chuckling by now.

"You've been had love. I think this pair have cottoned onto your masterplan and are playing you at your own game."

"I thought it was too good to be true. I know I'm good but not that good!"

"Yep, you missed your true vocation Lisa," laughed Richard.

Annie quickly moved to Lisa's side and put an arm around her. "If only I had a camera, your face was a picture."

"Alright you lot, enough jokes at my expense. Let's go through while we wait on dinner. You two can tell me exactly what other cunning plans you have up your sleeve."

As they made their way through, Annie could not help but cast a sly glance at Richard. The kiss had not been planned, only the hug, although she wasn't complaining. It had been a very nice kiss.

"Don't let Lisa see you looking like that, she might get the wrong idea," whispered Dan in her ear as he walked past into the living room.

Annie smiled, perhaps tonight was going to be even more

enjoyable than she had originally thought.

Chapter Fourteen

The following morning, Annie woke up to the room filled with a blinding whiteness that only a snowfall could produce. She had not bothered to close the curtains when she finally got to bed last night. The sky had been so full of snow and she had enjoyed lying in bed watching the silent snowfall as she slowly drifted off to sleep.

Last night had been fun. Dan had so obviously enjoyed having another man around to chat to, and the evening had been filled with laughter as they recounted old stories. There had been no awkwardness with Richard and he had stayed much longer than Annie had expected him to. He had been great at keeping the evening going and Lisa had positively glowed all night.

Annie could feel her throat start to tighten just thinking about the significance of today. As if on cue Bonnie came charging through the door and launched herself onto Annie's bed.

Dan tapped on the door and poked his head through.

"Sorry Annie, Bonnie couldn't wait any longer to come in. Breakfast is on and should be ready in ten minutes."

"Thanks Dan, be down in a minute," Annie grunted as she tried to push Bonnie off.

"God, this dog is even heavier than yesterday. Have you been feeding her extras while I've been asleep?"

"No, you are totally to blame for your dog's girth," laughed Dan as he headed back to the kitchen.

Annie grimaced, and after a few minutes of wrestling with Bonnie she finally managed to writhe her way out of the bed. Slipping on a t-shirt and a pair of jogging bottoms, Annie splashed some cold water on her face. The smell of bacon cooking was wafting upstairs and she could hear the faint strains of a Christmas tune playing from the radio. By now, Bonnie was almost hopping from paw to paw in anticipation of getting some leftovers from breakfast.

"Come on fattie, let's see what they have laid out for us."

Coming into the kitchen, Annie caught sight of the Christmas tree, which now seemed to have an increased pile of presents under it compared to last night. This could only mean that Lisa had been buying even more tacky Christmas gifts. Annie gave a wry smile and shook her head, "Lisa, what have you been up to?"

"You'll see. Breakfast first though."

Dan placed a huge pile of bacon in the middle of the kitchen table along with some bread rolls, "Help yourself Annie".

She couldn't believe how hungry she felt, especially after such a large meal the night before. Bonnie's tail thumped on the floor as Annie waggled a rasher of bacon in front of her. "Come on then, it is Christmas after all," before she had even finished her sentence, Bonnie had bounded over and downed the rasher in one go.

"Very impressive. She left you any fingers?"

"Yep, still intact," and as if to prove the point, Annie waggled her fingers in front of her face.

"I think my lovely wife has been up to no good during all these hours on her own in the house. Have you seen the tree? I dread to think what we are going to unwrap today."

"I can hear you both, I'm not deaf you know!"

Dan and Annie laughed, "We've been caught."

"Come on you two, join me on the sofa and we can get started on the presents."

Grabbing a tray laden with mugs, milk, sugar as well as an industrial sized teapot, Annie headed through. The coal fire was ablaze and Lisa had placed a bowl of oranges studded with cloves close by. The smell of the fire combined with the warm oranges was so homely and reassuring. Just like any normal Christmas, thought Annie.

Bonnie was splayed out in front of the fire and Annie had to step over her as there was no way on earth that she was going to budge. Lisa looked tired but Annie knew better than to say anything. She knew how much Lisa had enjoyed last night and Annie and Dan had already acknowledged that Lisa would be tired today. They had both agreed that as long as she was happy and comfortable, they would not nag her. Just keep a watchful eye on her.

"So, are you ready for your presents?"

"Lisa, I dread to think what you have done this year."

A small smile played on her lips, as she looked at them both, "Such suspicious minds."

Dan was charged with the job of handing out the gifts. He handed a large flat parcel to Annie. "Good luck!" he joked.

Looking at the tag, all it had written on it was, 'memories, me xx'. Her stomach lurched, this was going to be even harder than she thought. Carefully taking off the paper revealed a large picture frame that had been filled with photographs of the three of them from childhood through to more recent times. Dates and locations along with a comment about each photograph had been carefully written out. As Annie scanned them, she came across one of her with Bonnie as a puppy. A posed photo of Lisa and Annie at a school dance in what they had thought at the time was the must-have fashion. One picture that caught her eye was of the three of them taken six months ago. Just a day before they had found out that Lisa's cancer had come back.

"Lisa, it's perfect. Thank you so much."

"I thought, that on days when you are feeling low and I'm not there to nag you, that you could look at this and if nothing else, laugh at Dan's hairstyle when he was at high school!"

They both laughed as Dan pulled a grimace, "Always the butt of your jokes, aren't I?"

"Oh you love it," laughed Annie.

Dan handed a small parcel to Lisa, "I know you said that you didn't want any presents love but I thought you would like this."

Lisa had instructed them both that they were not to buy her anything this year but, as usual, neither of them had listened to her. Opening her present revealed packets of snowdrop, crocus and daffodil bulbs.

"I know it's late for planting but let's aim for us all seeing these flower in the spring."

Annie knew that there was significance to his sentiments and she watched as Lisa went very quiet and still.

Looking up at them both Lisa whispered, "I'll try my best Dan."

A silence lay between them all at what this present symbolised. From its simplicity of spring flowers Dan was aiming for a milestone to keep Lisa alive. While at the same time, for the first time, he was vocally acknowledging what would be the inevitable conclusion.

"Right, let's get this present giving back on track. Dan, can you start handing out the ones at the front please."

"Oh lord," muttered Annie.

After ten minutes of unwrapping some of the worst presents that she had ever seen, which now resulted in Bonnie being dressed in pink lacy booties and a mop cap. Annie handed over her present to Lisa. Shaking her head at Annie, Lisa opened her gift and holding the small, delicate necklace up to the light of the fire, she stared at Annie with tears in her eyes.

"Oh Annie, it's beautiful."

"Do you want me to put it on for you?"

Lisa nodded. It was the first time in a long time that she had let her emotions break through in front of either of them. Carefully placing it around her neck, Annie planted a kiss on top of Lisa's head, "It's still not as beautiful as you."

"Hear, hear," agreed Dan.

"I love it Annie, thank you. Dan, there is one more present under the tree for Annie. Can you get it out for me please?"

"Oh god Lisa, I don't think I can take any more mugs with naked men on them," laughed Annie.

Dan handed it over to Annie. The gift tag had written on it, 'to my psychic buddy. You'll know when I'm around'. Ripping open the paper, Annie found nestled within a large mound of tissue paper, a wind-chime.

"Keep it in the house Annie. When I come to visit you'll hear me," whispered Lisa, just loud enough for Annie to hear. Annie nodded, unable to speak.

"Good girl, stiff upper lip, remember," Lisa squeezed her hand.

"Right Dan, it's time we got ourselves washed, dressed and fully medicated."

Only Lisa could make light of her situation. They all laughed.

"Annie, you might want to take that stuff off of Bonnie before she slips on the floor."

Bonnie snorted as if in agreement.

Chapter Fifteen

It was early evening and Lisa had finally admitted that
she was tired and had reluctantly headed up to bed for
some sleep. Dan had fallen asleep in front of the fire after
all the festivities, which now left Annie and Bonnie at a
loose end.

It had stopped snowing, so it seemed like the ideal
opportunity for a short walk and to let Bonnie do what
nature intended. Pulling one of Lisa's woolly hats on as
she walked out of the front door, the coldness of the air
took Annie's breath away. Bonnie was trying to back-up
into the doorway and head for the fire.
"Not a chance Bonnie. You need to 'do your stuff'
otherwise I won't let you back in."
Pulling the hat down over her ears, they headed down the
street. It was cold but Annie felt in need of a long walk so
had decided to walk through the town and then circle
round in the direction of the beach. Bonnie reluctantly
followed behind. As they walked past houses, Annie
could not help but sneak a look in through the windows.

Christmas trees were ablaze with fairy lights, and the familiar blue flicker of televisions being watched bounced off the walls. Everything appeared normal for everyone else. No life-changing moments. No psychic visions for the residents of these houses. Annie bowed her head, the cold making her tears sting her cheeks as they fell. Her familiar life was about to change and there was absolutely nothing she could do about it. The ache she felt in her chest was overwhelming. Just how would her life be without Lisa? How would Dan be after Lisa was gone, would he be able to cope? Could he ever be happy again? Lisa was his whole life and he would need all of Annie's help but Annie desperately needed someone as well. Bonnie was a good companion but she could not exactly talk things through with Annie to help her.

She had been so caught up in her thoughts that Annie had not been paying attention to where she was walking. Suddenly, she walked into something, or rather someone. Lifting her head up, ready to apologise her eyes widened when she saw that she had bumped into Richard. He took one look at her and without saying anything, wrapped his arms around her and drew her into him. She must have sobbed for at least ten minutes and not once did he say anything. He just held her gently and stroked her back.

Finally, Annie pulled back, "Sorry."

"Hey, that was a long time coming. Do you want to walk and talk for a bit?"

Annie nodded, still not totally confident that she could trust herself not to cry again, then she realised that she had not seen Bonnie. As if reading her mind, Richard pointed his finger towards the beach.

"It's okay, she's over there playing with Dexter."

"Dexter?"

"Yep, I take no account for the name. Mum got a lab last year from the rescue place down the road. Her and Dad are sleeping off Christmas dinner so I thought I'd bring him down here and we could both get a breath of fresh air." He smiled at Annie, as he wiped away the last of her tears, "Got too much eh?"

She nodded. As she watched the dogs chasing each other, she felt relieved that she had let some of the pent up emotion out.

"Do you want to walk down to the shore and join our furry friends?"

"That would be good thanks, although I'll need to start heading back soon. I left Lisa and Dan sleeping. If they wake up and I'm not there, they'll send out a search party."

"No problem, how about we head back up the beach towards their house and then I'll know that you're home safe. It also means that by the time I get Dexter home, he will be well and truly knackered!"

They both laughed, "If you're sure you are okay going out of your way, then that would be really lovely."

They walked along the shoreline in amiable silence. Both of them lost in their own thoughts but enjoying each other's company all the same. Finally, Richard broke the silence.

"You never did tell me how you knew about things that I had never talked about the other day."

Annie dug her hands deeper into her pockets, 'what the hell' she thought. He'd seen her cry her eyes out so why not just tell him the truth. Taking a deep breath she decided to take the plunge. "Well, I'm what you would call a psychic medium." She waited for the laughter, but none came.

"Explain."

So far so good, thought Annie. "Well, I see and hear things but I mainly work from feelings and emotions. I know it sounds really weird but I'm not mad, I promise you."

"Well, to be fair Annie, you were always a bit of a fruit loop at high school."

"I prefer the term 'dizzy'."

He chuckled at her comment.

"You don't look shocked."

"I think I'm probably still trying to digest what you have just told me. Although I have to say, I don't feel that surprised by what you have just said which is a bit odd. So, out of curiosity, how did you come across the name of Lucy the other day?"

Annie threw a sideways look at him. "Aah, well, I did something that I don't usually do."

"Oh yes?" Another raised eyebrow. He really was quite practised at those, thought Annie.

"I have a rule, that I do not try anything with friends."

"Try anything? What do you mean exactly?"

Annie thought for a moment. It was always really difficult for her to explain what she did in a way that made sense and she felt that she owed Richard, at the very least, a decent explanation.

"Okay, think back to when you met someone new at work for example. I bet you had the usual thing of being introduced to them. Probably shook their hand, and exchanged some banal conversation for a couple of minutes.

"Well, I'm with you so far."

Annie wasn't sure if he was being sarcastic but she carried on regardless. "I want you to remember the last time that happened."

"Well, funnily enough, it was about six weeks ago. I've got a new assistant and to be honest, I reckon he's a total pratt."

"But why do you think that?" It was Annie's turn to raise an eyebrow.

"Well, he just is. I can't put my finger on it but he's just got that air about him."

"Exactly! You don't know it for definite but your gut-instinct has kicked in," Annie paused for a moment to let it sink in. "Your gut instinct is, to me, your unconscious mind telling you, or even warning you, about something. The trick is listening and understanding it."

"Are you telling me that your gut instinct told you about the name Lucy?"

"No, not totally. What I'm trying to do is explain the basics here. I'll take a look at someone and my gut instinct will give me a heads-up as to how, or even what, that person is feeling. When we were in the cemetery and you were stroking Bonnie, I took the opportunity to see how you were feeling. As I looked at you I felt sad, and then the name Lucy came into my head."

"So, you are telling me, that just by looking at me, that you got that?"

Annie nodded, she could tell that she was not making a good job of explaining things. Suddenly, she had a brainwave. "Right, I'm going to show you how to see an aura."

"You have got to be joking Annie. We're on a beach, it's dark and you've just told me that you have a severe case of the Derek Acorah's"

She chose to ignore his sarcasm and stood in front of him.

"Do you remember the Ready brek ads?"

"What, the ones with the boy in his duffle coat, going to school?"

Annie nodded. "What do you remember about the boy?"

"Well, he had that red glow around him, to show that he had eaten his breakfast. Although, I have to say I never thought it was that tasty myself."

"You're going off the point now. Go back to that red glow."

"What! Are you telling me I look like the Ready Brek kid?"

"Not quite, but the way I see auras is similar to that glow around his body. To start off with, it's white but then I'll see colours in amongst it. The thing is, everyone can see auras if they try."

"Yeh, right."

"Seriously, you can...." Annie's phone rang.

"You have got to get that ring tone changed."

Ignoring him she answered the phone, "I'm on the beach walking Bonnie. Yes, I know it's dark but I'm fine." Richard was smirking at her. He knew that she would not want to say that she was with him, as Lisa would be off on her matchmaking again. He coughed loudly and smirked at Annie, who threw him a look to kill.

"Yes, that was a male cough you heard. No, it's not a stranger."

"Hi Lisa!" Richard shouted.

At this point, Annie looked ready to throttle him, "She wants to say hello." She almost threw the phone at him. After a couple of minutes, he handed the phone back to Annie who quickly said goodbye and hung up.

Richard took hold of her hand. "Don't be angry Annie. It was just too good an opportunity to miss. I know what Lisa can be like and it was funny seeing the look on your face. Come on, I can see their house from here, let me walk you back," he held up his hands as if in surrender. "I'd like to hear more about what you were talking about. I'm not saying I believe it but I am curious."

She looked up at him. He was smiling at her but not laughing, which was a bonus.

"Okay. I'm absolutely freezing now anyway so it would be good to get back. Where are the dogs?"

After couple of minutes of whistling, they appeared from further up the beach.

"I hope you've behaved yourself Dexter. Out with a lady at this time of night, what would the parents say?" Both of the dogs raced ahead of them as they made their way back towards Lisa's house and Annie could see the silhouette of Lisa at her bedroom window.

"Welcoming party is out I see," teased Richard.

"No thanks to you,' Annie joked back.

He stopped and turned her round to look at him, "Are you okay now? I know you've been finding it hard. She's your best friend Annie. I can't even begin to imagine how you are feeling. Any time you need to just talk, then you know where I am."

Annie nodded, her eyes glistening. "Thanks Richard, I do appreciate it. You know you're not going to get to escape without coming in?"

"I'd guessed that much. Are you okay with that?"

She nodded, "Yes I am."

Chapter 16

Karen sat very still, the only show of emotion was a
solitary tear rolling down her cheek. The baby growing
inside her letting its presence be known as it kicked out,
stretching tiny limbs.

"Come on Karen love, let's get you to bed. You're not
doing yourself or the little 'un, any good staying up all
night. If I hear anything then I'll wake you straight
away."

Karen stared at her father as if he was a stranger. It took
her a moment to focus on his mouth, seeing it moving,
before she realised that he was talking to her. She shifted
in her chair. Her back was aching and her legs felt like
lead. The last thing she felt like doing was getting up out
of the chair and going to bed.

"Where is he dad? Why hasn't he rung?" A sob caught
the back of her throat.

He shook his head, "I don't know love, it's certainly not
like Kevin but I'm sure there is a very simple explanation

and we'll all laugh about it in a couple of days time." He tried to give her a reassuring smile but failed miserably. "Look, why not go and have a bath and I'll try ringing his boss again to see if there is any news."

She looked up at him wearily and nodded. He was just going to fuss around her and at least if she was in the bath she could shut the door and be alone with her thoughts. As she slowly walked up the stairs, she could feel his eyes watching her with each step she took.

As soon as the bathroom door closed behind her, he picked up the phone and hit redial.

"Hi, it's Geoff again, any news?"

"Sorry Geoff, we've tried all the regular contacts we have out there but nobody seems to have seen Kevin since he went to have a couple of days break on Gozo. We've spoken to the local police again, but to be honest, they're not being all that helpful."

Geoff gave a resigned sigh, "I just don't understand it. He's such a reliable lad, I don't think that he would do this just to upset Karen. There has to be another reason. Have all the local hospitals been checked?"

"Yep, still no record of him being admitted. I think it's time we got the British Police involved. It's been forty-eight hours now and like you, I agree that this is not normal behaviour from Kevin. Do you want me to ring them?"

"If you don't mind, that would be great. I don't want Karen getting any more upset. If she hears me on the phone to the police it will just set her off again."

"No problem, I'll contact a close friend of mine who is fairly high up in the force. Hopefully I can call in a favour and get them to act quickly on this, especially given the fact it's Christmas."

"Keep me posted on what he says. I don't like the fact that no-ne has heard from Kevin. I know that the pair of them have had a few issues lately but nothing that would stop him coming home. Something's not right here and we need help, quickly."

"I'll ring you, as soon as I hear anything."

Putting down the phone, Geoff steadied himself against the back of a chair. He was tired and feeling the strain of trying to keep up a front for Karen. If only Molly were still alive. The girl needed her mum. Damn it, he needed his wife. She would have known what to do and what to say. He was just making a mess of it all and felt as if he was treading on eggshells. Taking a deep breath, he relaxed his grip from the chair. The light-headedness had gone, he'd make them both some tea, at least he could do that without making a mess of things.

Chapter 17

"So, what were you two up to on the beach last night? You were very quiet after he left, is everything alright?"

"What you really want to know is, did we get up to anything? I think Bonnie probably got more action than I did!"

"So, you admit it. You do like him!" A smug smile crept across Lisa's face.

"That is not what I said and you know it. Stop jumping to the wrong conclusion! We just chatted and talked about how you and Dan can't handle the pace anymore," Annie laughed as she dodged the cushion being thrown in her direction.

"Now ladies, what's going on in here? I go out for half an hour and come back to flying missiles," Dan squeezed Annie's shoulders as he walked past her. "Nice moonlit walk along the beach last night then?"

She threw him a look, "Oh for God's sake don't you start as well!"

"Well, we like a bit of excitement and intrigue in our lives these days, don't we love?"

"We sure do," giggled Lisa. "It's what keeps us going."

Annie shook her head at the pair of them. "How about doing something constructive, like going over the notes I've made so far about this dream I've been having."

"Ah, she's using the distraction technique. What do you reckon Lisa, is she trying to hide something from us?"

"Without a doubt. The question is do we let her get away with it?"

"If you two don't stop this, I'll pack my bag and go home early."

"Okay, okay, I'll make a coffee. Can't have you storming out, we wouldn't have any entertainment."

Lisa patted the sofa, "Come on then, lets see what you've got so far."

Annie brought out her notes. They still did not make up the picture she so desperately wanted. She was hoping that between the three of them, they might be able to make sense of what she had so far.

Lisa took a brief look at the notes, "I've got an old roll of wallpaper in the cupboard. Why don't you grab it and we can write out the list on the back of it and hang it up for inspiration."

Annie rummaged around in the cupboard until she found the roll as well as some blue tac.

"Are you sure about sticking it up on the wall?"

Lisa nodded, "Put it by the window then I can see it from where I'm sat without having to strain my neck."

Balancing precariously on a chair, Annie dutifully stuck up the roll of paper, just as Dan came back into the room.

"Redecorating now are we?" He sat next to Lisa and picked up the notes that Annie had left.

"I thought Annie could put up the list in a place that I can see without having to fumble through lots of pieces of paper."

"Good idea. You always were the brains of the operation!" Dan smiled, glad to see that Lisa was getting involved in something. He had not told Annie yet about the bad night that Lisa had. Lisa had pleaded with him not to say anything but they both knew that he would.

For now he would let the girls enjoy themselves while keeping a watchful eye on her.

"Okay, let's go over the first few things here on your notes Annie. You've written down about the smell of the sea. Are you sure that you didn't have a window open?"

Annie did not take offence at the question. She knew that Lisa was helping her to eliminate anything that could be an outside influence. She shook her head.

"No, with the weather turning so cold, I've got all the windows shut. If this had happened in the middle of summer, it might have been a different story."

"Okay, the ring. What can you remember about it?"

Annie squeezed her eyes shut, trying to remember her last vision. "It had an engraving on it. I just can't make it out properly, I think it may have been a crown but I'm not one hundred percent sure. There was definitely a green stone in the middle of it, I remember the flash of colour against the gold of the ring."

"The azure window. That rings a bell. Dan, do you know what that is?"

"Let me check on the computer. You girls carry on, I'll see what I can dig up on the good old world wide web." He picked up his coffee and ambled off towards the study, muttering away to himself about mad women and psychics. The girls laughed.

"You know he enjoys it, don't be fooled by his mutterings and moanings. So, while he's off looking at the Azure Window, what else do you have?"

Annie wrote up her notes on the wallpaper and sat next to Lisa, "I'm really worried about the fact that they have the wrong person. I just don't understand what it means but I do know in my gut that he is in serious trouble and it is a case of mistaken identity." She lay down on the sofa with her head resting on Lisa's lap. A familiar position when Annie was struggling with one of her psychic puzzles. Lisa combed her fingers through Annie's hair just as a mother would, to calm an upset child. As Lisa reviewed the list, she could not help but wonder at how Annie coped with all of these visions and emotions that came with her psychic ability. It had always amazed her that someone so down-to-earth as Annie could have an ability that was continually under scrutiny. She had seen Annie struggle to keep it together, with some of the more serious experiences that had come her way. She could still remember vividly the time that Annie had collapsed with pains in her chest after talking to a woman who had come into the flower shop. All the time that she had been in the shop, Annie had been in severe pain but had held it together somehow until she had left. With tears streaming down her cheeks she had gasped for breath and managed to whisper to Lisa that the woman had been a victim of a stabbing. Lisa had been sceptical as the woman seemed fine to her, but she knew that Annie would not make it up. A week later, Lisa found out that the woman's son had been stabbed to death through the chest. Annie had picked up on him and what was to come. It had left her shaken and unsure if she wanted to carry on letting these visions through but with the support of both Lisa and Dan, she had worked her way through her mixed emotions and was able to separate her experiences much better than before.

"Well, I'll be damned. She's done it again!" Dan came through from the study waving a print out in front of him.

Annie had drifted off to sleep but quickly sat upright on hearing Dan.

"What have you found Dan?" Annie was trying to reach up and grab the paper from his hand but he held it too high for her to reach.

"Annie, I'm sure you are shrinking or have you always been a short-arse!"

"Just because you're built like the Jolly Green Giant! Now let me see what you've got!"

Lisa shook her head, "Will you two ever grow up?"

Dan and Annie looked at one another and smiled. "Nope," they chorused.

"Well, if you don't mind, I'm going to leave you two kids together as I need to have a lie down." She shot them both a look. "Don't even think of starting to fuss. I'm just tired and need a couple of hours to recharge my batteries."

Neither of them were convinced by Lisa's show of bravado but they both knew better than to argue with her. Dan was the first to speak after she left the room. "She didn't have a good night last night. The pain was a lot worse than usual but she wouldn't let me call anyone or even wake you up."

"You should have told me Dan, I wouldn't have started on this if I'd known."

"But that's what she wants. Just a bit of normality, for just a little bit longer. I realise that now." He sat down beside Annie, still with the print out in his hands. She took it off him and put it to one side.

"Come here Dan," she wrapped her arms around him and let him rest his head on her shoulder. The only indication that he was giving in to the tears was the heaving of his shoulders as he sobbed silently. She gently rocked him, not daring to say anything in fear of breaking down herself.

"I'm sorry Annie. I just want her to stay here with me. With us. I don't want it to change but I can't stop this. I feel so bloody useless."

She ruffled his hair. "We both do Dan but we have to face up to the fact that we can't stop what is happening. All we can do is make sure that Lisa has as much fun as she can in the time left, and is as comfortable as possible. It was never going to be easy but we've both got to face up to the fact that she isn't going to be with us much longer. I so want to make all of this go away but I can't. I'll do everything I can to be here for both of you. You are my family and I just can't bear to see you both suffering."

"Will you do something for me?"

"Anything."

"Move in with us?"

"Oh Dan, we've talked about this before. You both need time on your own, the last thing you need is me here all the time. I come every day anyway so it's not as if I'm a million miles away."

"But that's just it! You come every day so why not just stay with us? She needs you Annie. I need you. It's only going to get harder and nights like last night are going to become more frequent. You know how stubborn she is about going into hospital, we have everything prepared here for when she gets worse. Stay with us, please?"

Annie was torn. On the one hand, she knew that it made sense, but she also didn't want to get in the way. Dan grabbed her hands, desperation in his eyes.

"Annie, I can't do this on my own anymore. Please help me."

This was the first time that he had openly admitted to how he really felt. How could she say no? He was like a brother to her. She sighed, knowing all along that it would come to this and that she would give in. She had just hoped that it would not be quite so soon, as it could mean only one thing. Lisa was getting worse.

Chapter **18**

"Are you sure you're up to doing this love? I'm sure the police could do this without you needing to upset yourself anymore."

Karen nodded, uncomfortable in the brightly lit surroundings. The camera lights were incredibly bright and she felt disoriented by them. Journalists from local and national television were joggling for a position in front of her.

"I'll be fine Dad. The police said that it would help if I said a few words, I think they called it the sympathy vote." She shook her head. It was now New Years Eve and there was still no word or sighting of Kevin. It was as if he had just disappeared off the planet.

"Mrs Lyons, are you ready for the press conference?" The young female constable held out her hand to help Karen out of her chair and lead her to the main table where already several police officers were seated in preparation.

"Dad, you are coming with me?" The look of panic on Karen's face made Geoff want to take her home. Surely

108

they could do this without her. The young constable gave him a knowing look, they had already discussed the benefits of Karen speaking to the press. There would be much more widespread coverage if the young, pregnant wife spoke rather than a police spokesperson.

"Of course I am love, try stopping me." He took her arm and they slowly made their way to the waiting cameras and microphones.

Chapter 19

"Annie, Dan, get in here now!"

They looked at one another with fear in their eyes and rushed through into the living room where Lisa lay on the sofa. The past couple of nights had seen her in much more pain, so they had insisted that she rest on the sofa with Bonnie keeping her company, while they prepared dinner.

"What's wrong love? Are you in pain?"

"Lisa, what is it?"

"Oh for goodness sake you two, shut up and listen to the telly will you!" Lisa turned up the volume. Dan and Annie looked at one another, puzzled but relieved that at least there was nothing wrong. They sat on either end of the sofa to watch what Lisa was pointing at.

"Oh," was all that Annie could manage.

In front of her was a young pregnant woman making an emotional plea for her missing husband. She was holding up a picture of him and obviously trying to keep it together as she spoke.

"This is a photo of Kevin taken just three months ago. If anyone has seen this man can they please contact the police. He was due back from Malta just before Christmas but he has not been seen, or been in contact with anyone, since December 21st. Please help me find my husband." The camera zoomed into the photo. A dark, curly haired young man smiled back at them. Annie's eyes drifted down the picture, a red sweat top with lettering and blue trainers with a yellow stripe.

"Shit!" was all Dan could manage.

"Very eloquent Dan. Annie, are you okay?" Lisa reached out to grab her hand.

The doorbell rang and they all jumped.

"I'll get it. You girls need to think about what we're going to do."

Annie shook her head and whispered, "Lisa, we can't do anything. You know what it's like when the police are involved. They end up making the psychic look like the guilty party."

"Don't worry Annie, we'll work out what's best here," Lisa gave an encouraging squeeze of her hand.

"Look what the cat's dragged in!" Dan moved aside to let in Richard.

"I hope you don't mind me popping round. The parents aren't doing much for New Year's Eve so I thought I would stop by and say hello and see what you were all up to." He looked at the three of them with a puzzled expression. "Either my new aftershave isn't as appealing as I thought or you three have just seen a ghost." He looked in Annie's direction, "Actually, knowing Annie as I now do, perhaps you have."

Dan cleared his throat trying to disguise a laugh. "Very good, mate. Think you may have scored an own goal with the girls though, but good pun."

Now that he was fully in the lounge, he could see the roll of wallpaper with all of Annie's notes on it. "What's all this? Is it a new type of charades?"

Lisa made to sit up but Annie and Dan motioned for her to stay where she was, which did not go unnoticed by Richard.

"Have I come at a bad time?"

"No, not at all. I'm sorry Richard, we've been a bit taken aback by something that was just on the television. Dan, why don't you get Richard a beer." She took a look at Annie. "I think perhaps Annie could do with a whisky."

"Coming right up m'lady. Come on through with me Richard, I'll fill you in while I get the drinks."

Lisa waited until the men had left the room and then turned her attention to Annie. "You've not said anything Annie. What are you thinking?"

"I'm thinking, now it's real. Until now, it was just a bad dream and some visions but now it has a life. I don't know what to do."

"Well, we need to just think this through tonight. Perhaps we should work a bit more on your notes and see if we can get anything else?"

Richard and Dan came back into the room, armed with drinks and a big bowl of popcorn. Lisa smiled, it was a bit of a ritual, that while they were working on one of Annie's puzzles, that they would break out the popcorn and sit around until the early hours talking through what they had uncovered. It seemed fitting that Richard was here as well. The threesome of herself, Annie and Dan was going to be one short soon enough. Maybe it was time to let someone new come into the group and learn the ropes. She sat up and made a shushing noise when Annie and Dan started to tell her to lie down. "I'm fine, sitting up is not going to cause a relapse so just be quiet. Richard, why don't you come and sit next to me, while we initiate you into BALDI's."

"BALDI's?"

"Oh god," groaned Annie, "this is embarrassing."

Lisa laughed, "You mean you have never heard of the investigation team BALDI's?"

"Now I know you're playing with me. Come on play fair."

Dan came to his rescue. "It's short for Bonnie, Annie, Lisa and Dan Investigations. Admittedly the name was born during some rather drunken circumstances but it's stuck so we affectionately call ourselves the BALDI's."

"Well, you learn something new every day. But what would happen if I joined the group?"

"We'd be BALDIR!" they laughed.

Chapter 20

The four of them had spent the past hour going over Annie's notes. All the time, Lisa and Dan pushed Annie harder. Questioning her dreams and feelings. Pushing her for what they knew would be the key to the puzzle but was still buried deep within her subconscious. Richard had kept quiet and observed. Occasionally, he would chip in with a question but for the rest of the time he listened and watched what went on around him.

Annie excused herself for what she termed a 'nature break' and Dan used the opportunity to pour them another drink.

"How does she do it Lisa?" Richard was staring intently at the wallpaper list, "I had no idea that when she said she was a psychic medium, that it entailed all this."

"What did you think? That she told fortunes and occasionally saw Great Aunt Matilda in the corner of the room?" mused Lisa.

"I suppose in some way, yes! I knew about the emotional and feelings side. She told me about that the other day but until you actually see it in action.....well, it sort of takes your breath away. I'm not sure that I could handle all of those emotions as well as she does."

"Well, there was a point where she nearly gave it all up. It did get too much for her. She used to let herself get far too emotionally involved. I'm not saying that she doesn't now, but she can separate the two, which is a much healthier way to handle it. Although, on saying that, now she knows that there is a pregnant wife in the mix, she's going to push herself harder to find that missing piece."

"Right ladies and gent, coffee to keep us all awake." Dan was carrying through a tray, precariously laden with cups, caffetiere and a mound of biscuits. "By the way, we have an hour until midnight folks. What say we take a few strides from the backdoor to the beach and watch the fireworks?"

"Excellent idea, although are you going to be okay Lisa?" Richard knew from what Dan had briefly told him earlier, that she had not been so good. It worried him that perhaps they were pushing her too far, just staying up as late as they were, going over Annie's notes.

"I'm fine. It keeps my mind off things and besides, someone needs to show you the ropes if you're going to become part of our team."

He laughed, running a hand through his hair, "Baldi by name but not by nature."

Annie observed the scene from her position by the doorway. Dan was playing at his usual good host act when what he was really doing, was keeping his hands and mind occupied. Lisa looked tired, and there were dark circles under her eyes that were obviously down to the bad episodes of the past few nights as well as the medication. Richard looked at ease amongst what was anything but a normal evening with friends. How long would it last, she wondered. He did seem to be taking it all in his stride but it would be good to know what he was really thinking.

As if sensing being watched, Richard turned towards her. Smiling, he held out his hand and beckoned her over. "Come on Annie, we have a puzzle to solve and you need to get these two back on track."

Returning his smile, she walked over and sat on the floor

by his feet. Reaching over to pick up her mug of coffee,

she suddenly stopped, with her hand in mid-air.

Concerned, Richard leaned over, "Annie! Are you

okay?"

Lisa gestured to Richard to keep quiet. She knew that

Annie was probably seeing or feeling something.

Whispering to Richard, so as not to disturb Annie, "She's

okay, just think of it as she is having a senior moment and

can't remember what it was that she was supposed to do!"

She was trying to make light of what would be for Annie,

a confusing experience. She had tried to explain to Lisa in

the past, that at times like these, it would be as if someone

had just turned on a television in her head and that the

clarity would only last a moment, before it would be

suddenly switched off again.

Annie shook her head and grabbed her coffee. Swigging a

mouthful, she looked around at them all staring at her,

"What?"

"Come on, what did you see?"

"It's going to sound stupid."

"Annie, you know by now that you can't let how you feel about these things get in the way. Say what you get, remember?"

"Anyway Annie," chuckled Dan, "you're not going to look any less stupid than normal."

"Thanks mate," Annie leaned over and playfully punched his arm. "If you're going to be Mr Smarty Pants, you can do the writing." Unconsciously, she leaned back against Richard's legs. It did not go unnoticed by Dan or Lisa. A small, satisfied sigh escaped from Lisa's lips.

Clapping his hands together, Dan stood up, pen at the ready. "Okay, what have you got?"

"Like I said, I know it will sound stupid. It's almost like a name. Victoria Rabit."

Dan snorted, "Victoria Rabit! Did you have a swift swig of whisky when you went to the loo?"

"Write it up Dan," scolded Lisa.

"Yes Miss."

As he wrote, Annie continued, "The blue water I saw. It's important. It's as if that's where he is now."

"What! He's in the water?"

119

"No," Annie shook her head, "It's as if the water is significant in how it looks. Almost as if it's saying, 'Come in'. I know it sounds daft but that is where the building with the blue door is." She looked around them all and cleared her throat. "There is one other thing."

Dan stopped writing and turned his attention to Annie. The tone of her voice had become more serious.

"Come on Annie, you know the rules. No keeping anything back."

She nodded, "Like I say. Some of it may be nonsense but I keep getting a connection with Kevin and the word paedophile but remember I said that they had the wrong person? Well, that's what I feel has happened. They think Kevin is the paedophile but he isn't."

The room fell silent.

"Crikey Annie. If that is the case, then this guy needs our help and quickly." Dan put down his pen.

Lisa broke the silence. "Right. I think we all need a break from this to clear our heads, plus it's nearly midnight. Dan, can you get my coat, hat and scarf please? Annie, Richard - there are some fireworks in the utility room.

How about you go and get them and then we will bring in
the New Year with a bang!"

As they all went about their tasks, Lisa sat back and
stared at the list. They would need to act on this, but how?
Annie would not want any involvement with police but
they would need to do something. She needed to think
how she could persuade her friend to do the one thing that
she knew she would be unhappy with, and that was, share
her information with the authorities.

Chapter 21

From Kevin's confined space in the small wooden hut, he could feel the cold air rushing through the cracks in the wood. As he looked up through a small slit in the roof, the sky was as clear as he had ever seen it. Velvet black with sparkling diamonds. Unfortunately he was not in the best of venues for appreciating the view.

He tried to move his legs but the pain in his right thigh shot through the whole of his body, causing him to retch. He had not eaten for days and the slightest movement made him feel nauseous and dizzy. He wasn't sure how long he had been here, or even if the two men were coming back.

He still could not work out what had happened. After his call with Karen, he had decided to go for a walk and clear his head. The feeling of being watched had continued to haunt him and not without good reason. He remembered that he had stopped to look behind him in an attempt to quash the feeling and felt a shot of panic rush through his body. Only fifty yards away there was a car parked up with the two men that had been observing him at the bar. He quickened his step, cursing the fact that he had picked such an isolated spot to walk off the beer and his confused and angry thoughts about Karen. He could hear the engine of the car revving and with one last quick glance over his shoulder he broke into a run. Unfortunately he had not been quick enough to out manoeuvre the car. A glancing blow had sent him flying and as his head hit the ground, his last conscious thought was, 'Why me?'

When he next woke, he realised that several hours must have passed since he had lost consciousness as it had now turned dark. His head ached from the impact but what frightened him more was the feeling of a rope around his neck. As he clawed at the rope, his captor tugged at it harder and pushed Kevin to what appeared to be the edge of a cliff. He had no idea how he had arrived there. Most importantly, he did not understand why these two men were doing this to him. He felt the rope tighten around his neck, the smell of stale sweat and cigarette smoke mixing with the salt spray that was being blown into his face, his fingers frantically searching for some small gap in the rope in an effort to relieve the pressure around his neck. Suddenly, there had been a large amount of shouting between his would be killer and his associate. As they had argued, Kevin had felt the rope loosen slightly so had tried to take advantage of the momentary loss of attention, to attempt an escape. The slippiness of the rocks combined with the darkness had resulted in him losing his footing. Ironically, it was the rope around his neck that had stopped his fall although not without damage. His neck was now red raw and he could not speak, due to the swelling of his throat. As the men had started to drag him back up the cliff face, his right thigh had been slashed deeply on the rocks.

He presumed that he must have passed out at this point, for the next thing he remembered was waking up in this small cramped hut. He felt weak, dehydrated, and his leg had become seriously infected. It was not looking good. All he could think about was Karen. The last time they had spoken, they had both said some very hurtful words to each other. 'Just let me live to tell her I love her' he thought, then blackness took over and his body slumped

against the wall of the hut. Unconscious again.

Chapter 22

"Happy New Year!" they all chorused. Dan lit the last rocket and they craned their necks in unison skywards as it shot high into the clear night sky and exploded into thousands of stars accompanied by an ear-shattering bang.

"Beautiful," sighed Lisa.

"Warm enough?" asked Dan as he wrapped his arms around her.

She nodded, "I am now. I love you Dan."

"I love you too. I just wish we had more time to grow old together."

"Me too."

He held her thin frame as tightly as he dared and they both looked up at the stars. "Do you think Annie's Kevin can see the stars from where he is?"

"I hope so, for all our sakes. She'll never forgive herself if she can't solve this one."

Dan swept Lisa up in his arms. "Come on you, it's far too cold for you to stay out here any longer," he chuckled as he lifted her, "you can still watch the lovebirds from inside the house."

"I was not watching."

"Yes you were, don't deny it." He carried her into the house and gently placed her on the sofa. Bonnie had not moved all the time that they had been outside.

"Has that dog got even lazier do you think?"

Lisa nodded, "It does seem that way doesn't it? It's either too much Christmas pudding or she's coming down with something. Annie's keeping an eye on her for now."

"I'll pour some whisky for when those two get back in. Why don't you have a look at that printout I brought through the other day? We never did read through it all and Annie was definitely right about the Azure Window. It makes you wonder what else she has got stuck in that messy little brain of hers!"

Lisa laughed at Dan's retreating back as she snuggled further down the sofa. She had to admit that she was feeling very tired, but at the same time, determined to see in her last New Year to the fullest. She had really appreciated the fact that Dan and Annie had kept their end of the bargain to keep everything as 'normal' as they could. She knew that they were distressed at the level of pain she was in and although Gordon their local GP had been doing a great job in keeping it under control, she was starting to worry herself about how bad it was getting, especially the past few nights. As she settled back, holding Dan's notes in one hand, Bonnie rose and positioned herself next to Lisa with her head resting on Lisa's lap as if looking for sympathy.

"What's up Bonnie, not feeling yourself?" Lisa stroked the top of Bonnie's head. "Go on, lie down here on the floor and then I can spoil you while the others aren't looking!" Bonnie lay down on the floor with her tail thumping half-heartedly, just as Dan came back into the room with a bottle of his favourite Bladnoch whisky and some glasses.

Lisa winked at him and laughed, "Oh, the Bladnoch! Seems fitting."

"Is Bonnie still pulling the sympathy vote then?"
"Yep seems like it," Lisa absent-mindedly carried on stroking Bonnie's head, "I'll mention it to Annie later.

Like I said, she's keeping an eye on her but she'd be heartbroken if anything was wrong with Bonnie. It's as if she is absolutely knackered. I know she's a lazy dog, but this is really unlike her."

"Unlike who?" asked Annie coming through into the living room. Her cheeks and nose were bright red with the cold and she had a sparkle in her eyes that neither Lisa nor Dan had seen in a long time.

"Bonnie. She still seems out of sorts."

Annie bent down and stared at her faithful companion, "What's up Bonns?"

Richard cleared his throat, "Erm, how long has she been like that?"

"Just the past few days, why?"

He looked sheepish. "It's obviously very early days but have you had her spayed?"

Annie shot him a look and jokingly covered Bonnie's ears. "No! What a question! Why?"

Richard smirked, "Well....." The raised eyebrow again she noted, "Dexter's never been neutered."

Dan burst out laughing. "Bloody hell Annie. Bonnie does get more action than you!"

Annie looked shocked. "You're kidding right? Anyway, that was only a week ago, it's far too early to tell."

Lisa couldn't stop laughing either, "Oh Annie, it could only happen to you and Bonnie. Give her a couple of weeks and if she is still out of sorts, take her to the vet's. Maybe I'll get to be an Aunty of sorts after all!"

Richard eyed the whisky, "Treating us Dan?"

"Don't get used to it!" Dan joked. He raised his glass in a toast, "To great loves and great friendships. To us!"

Tears pricked Annie's eyes as she raised her glass, "To us." She turned to Lisa, "To my best buddy and the bravest woman I have ever had the honour of calling my best friend. To Lisa!"

Lisa raised her glass to the threesome stood in front of her. Dan looked just as handsome as ever. Annie at long last had a spring in her step and a glow to her cheeks that was less to do with the cold and more to do with the budding relationship between her and Richard. She could not think of anywhere else she would rather be than here in her own home with the three of them. She looked across at Dan and smiled. "As you know, I am not one for speeches but there is something I would like to say. I am the luckiest woman alive. I have a wonderful husband, a fantastic best friend who both think nothing of what they have sacrificed for me over the past few months. Promise me that you will always look after one another." Dan and Annie nodded. Richard, who had kept himself at a slight distance, feeling almost like an intruder in such a personal and intimate moment, moved forward.

"I'd like to add my own toast if that's okay? To three most remarkable people who have shown me what true love and friendship really means. I feel truly privileged." They were all quiet for a moment. Each knew that the start of 2010 was the countdown for Lisa. She now refused any other treatment now apart from pain relief. Annie and Dan had both respected her wishes. They had seen how ill and distressed Lisa had become during her last bout of cancer treatment. She wanted to die with dignity and at home, which is what they had promised to let her do.

"Come on now, this is not how I want you all to remember our last New Year together. Richard, come over here and stop looking as if you feel like you're intruding!" teased Lisa.

"Well, maybe a bit. I did sort of gatecrash."

"Don't be daft man!" chipped in Dan. "We've all known each other for a long time. Just because you've gone and become a southerner doesn't mean that you can't be part of our family and, more importantly, the Baldis - remember!"

"Okay," Richard laughed, "To the Baldis."

They all raised their glasses, "The Baldis!" they chorused.

Chapter 23

Richard and Dan had decided to research Annie's place names on the laptop. Lisa was fast asleep on the sofa with Bonnie laid faithfully out on the floor beside her in front of the fire. Annie gently placed a blanket over her friend, being careful all the while not to wake her.

"Annie," whispered Richard, "I think I've found out who Victoria Rabit is." He had a slightly dazed look about him as he spoke to her.

Dan sat back, shaking his head, "Annie, you are not going to believe this."

"Come on guys, don't keep me waiting!" Annie was intrigued. She sat on the arm of the chair beside Richard so that she could see what he and Dan were looking at.

"Hang on," Dan rose out of his chair, "we need another piece of paper, this is important." He ripped off another piece from the roll that Annie had left by the window and hung it up with blu-tac next to the original draft. With black marker pen he wrote 'The Three Islands' along the top.

"Three islands?" questioned Annie.

"OK," sighed Dan, "bear with us. It will make sense in a minute."

Richard was still shaking his head. "Annie, I can't believe this."

"Oh come on, you are both scaring me now!"

"Sorry Annie, it's just thrown us both." Dan wrote on the paper the words 'Azure Window'. "This was one of your earliest signs wasn't it?" Dan nodded encouragingly at Annie, who nodded back.

"Yes, that's right. Thinking on, I never got to look at that printout of yours from the other day."

He wrote down 'Malta' and then turned to them both brandishing his marker pen in the air. "Okay, let's go back to the television appeal we saw earlier tonight. His wife mentioned Malta. Do you remember?"

Annie thought for a moment and then nodded, she could tell that Dan had got further down the path of joining up the pieces than she had. He sounded excited and she did not want to interrupt him.

He took a sip of his whisky, savouring the warmth as it trickled down his throat. He felt a certain excitement at what he and Richard had discovered but at the same time, he realised that this was going to lead to something bigger. He could feel it in the pit of his stomach, that old gut-instinct that Annie was always harping on about! He quickly glanced across to check on Lisa before he continued. She was still fast asleep, his sleeping beauty. Gathering his thoughts, he directed his attention back to Annie.

"So, we have the Azure Window and Malta. Now, if you were to look up the Azure Window on the internet, apart from the usual touristy stuff you will also discover that it can be found on the island of Gozo." He looked at Annie who just shrugged her shoulders. "Okay Annie, I know geography was never your strong point so listen carefully. The Azure Window is on a small island called Gozo," he drew a circle on the paper to represent the island. He then drew an asterix to the left of the circle, to indicate where the Azure Window was located. Looking at her, he wrote the initials VR in the centre of the circle.

"VR?" questioned Annie.

"Victoria Rabit," prompted Richard, "although what it correctly represents is the capital of Gozo which is called Victoria. A long time ago it used to be called Rabat, which means, 'the town', it's amazing how these things piece together isn't it?"

"Ah," nodded Annie, as she finally started to understand what the boys were trying to explain to her. "Victoria Rabit is a place, not a girl's name."

"Exactly!" Dan was sounding more excited by the minute.

"Well, I can see where you are going so far," encouraged Annie.

"Right, let's get you to the next point." Dan turned to write on the paper, which by now was becoming quite cramped with the amount of words and drawings. This time the words he wrote were 'Come In'.

Annie slumped back against the chair, folding her arms, "Dan I said that I didn't understand this."

"Hang on," Richard piped in, "listen to what he has to say."

Annie shrugged her shoulders, she had no idea where he was going with this now but Richard was right, she should hear out Dan's interpretation.

"Okay Annie. Remember you talked about the bluest water?"

She nodded.

"Well, there is a tiny island between Malta and Gozo called Comino. It has a natural attraction called the Blue Lagoon." He drew a representation of the three islands. "We know that Kevin was on Malta," Dan continued to draw, this time it was a dotted line which led towards the circle that he had marked as Gozo. "Let's assume that he then went to Gozo. Now, from here I think it's safe to assume from what you've said so far, that he probably went to Victoria and then to the Azure Window where we know from your dreams that something bad happened." He then drew a dotted line from Gozo to Comino. "I think that he was then taken to Comino where the Blue Lagoon is and that's where he is now!" He sat back, staring at Annie.

"Well, Annie?" even Richard was looking excited, "What do you think?"

She looked from her original notes to the drawings and notes that Dan had made. She shifted in her chair, looking at both of them. She could tell by their faces that they were both convinced by what they had said.

"Do you not think that the Comino link is a bit tenuous?"

"Annie, you should know better than that. Why are you stalling?"

Annie turned to where Lisa lay, "I thought you were asleep!"

"I have been awake long enough to hear what both Dan and Richard have said and it makes sense to me." She smiled gently at Annie, "Come on Annie, what does your gut instinct say?"

Annie looked around at them all. She gently stroked Bonnie's ear. She had to admit that what the boys had said did seem to make sense. She had also started to get that hot feeling all over her body, which she always experienced whenever she was close to something that was important. On top of that, there was the faintest

whiff of cigar smoke in the air around her.

She nodded at them all. "Okay. I'm in so far."

"Excellent!" Richard clapped his hands together.

"Enjoying this?" laughed Lisa.

"Well, when Annie said she was a psychic, I had no idea

that we would be playing Sherlock Holmes."

"Just remember one thing Watson!" interjected Annie.

"This is real. There is a pregnant woman looking for her

husband and we need to help her find him. Soon."

"So what now?" asked Richard. "Do we contact the

police with what we know?"

Annie shook her head, "It's really difficult with the

police. They either ignore you completely or assume that

in some way you must either be connected with the crime

or have inside information. I can appreciate that if it's

something you don't know about then you are bound to

be a bit suspicious. I just wish that they would listen a bit

more."

"Why don't we sleep on it tonight and then work out how

we approach this in the morning," suggested Lisa, "you

all look tired, Richard there's a spare bed if you want to crash here for tonight?"

"Thanks for the offer but I think a walk in the fresh air might help after all of Dan's whisky. Maybe another time," he winked at Lisa. He had really enjoyed feeling part of their very special family tonight. He motioned to get up and Annie rose with him.

"I'll see you out. I could do with a bit of air myself."

As they made their way out of the back door, Annie asked, "Are you walking back along the beach or keeping to the path?"

"I think I'll walk along the beach. It's such a beautiful night and I really miss being by the sea." He looked wistfully at the reflection of the moon in the water.

"Do you think you will ever come back here to stay?" quizzed Annie.

"Well, until recently I would have said no. I was settled job-wise, things were going well personally, or so I thought......" he tailed off.

"Do you mean with Lucy?" Annie held her breath, not sure if she had said too much.

He nodded, "Yes, with Lucy."

'He looks so sad' thought Annie. Whatever it was that had happened had obviously hurt him in a big way.

"It's a long story Annie, and I won't bore you with the details. I thought I had found someone that I wanted to spend the rest of my life with, however it appears that she would prefer to spend it with my best friend. At least I'm assuming that as the last time I saw them both, they were in my bed. I had been away at a conference but had got home earlier than planned and obviously before either of them had anticipated."

"Crikey Richard! I'm not quite sure what to say."

He laughed, "It's okay Annie. I won't deny that it doesn't still hurt but at least I found out before it was too late."

"How long ago did this happen?"

"Six months."

"Well, I'd say that it is still very early days to get over something like that," she smiled up at him hoping that he hadn't regretted saying anything about it.

"Thanks Annie. I've not told anyone up here about what went on. I feel a bit stupid about it all to be honest."

She nodded and put a finger to her lips, "Your secret is safe with me."

"Are you doing anything tomorrow?" he laughed, "I mean today don't I!"

"Well, I'm going over to my place to pick up some stuff and check on the house. I'm moving in now until..." she paused, unsure how to finish the sentence.

Richard nodded in understanding. "Dan did say that he had asked if you would move in. I think it's an excellent idea. Why not let me help you move some of your gear over?"

"Don't be daft! I'm sure you've got much better things to be doing with your time."

He grabbed hold of both her hands, "Annie, don't you understand that I would like to help. It would give me a chance to spend some time with you."

She shivered but it had nothing to do with the cold. It was completely to do with the pleasure of his touch and the warmth of his hands. He leaned down and kissed her forehead.

"Anyway, we still have the next part of your puzzle to solve. I'm finding it all very intriguing." He tilted up her chin and very gently placed a kiss on her lips. "Happy New Year Annie Murdoch."

The kiss was so gentle that she felt herself stretch up on tiptoe for more. He chuckled, "Bed for you. I'll pick you up at midday."

"Okay," she nodded.

He turned and headed off down the beach. 'Smooth devil', thought Annie but she couldn't help smiling all the same.

Chapter 24

Scuffling noises and hushed whispers roused Kevin slightly from his delirium. Although the weather was cooler than normal outside, Kevin's body was soaked in sweat. His leg had swollen to an alarming size and the smell rising from the open wound was sickening. He moved his head slightly but even that small movement caused another wave of dizziness and nausea. Slipping back into the blackness of unconsciousness, it was just as well that Kevin could not hear the conversation being held outside of his wooden prison.

The two men responsible for his injuries and attempted murder hovered outside the hut, peeking through the available slits in the wood. They were both shaking their heads. The fact that Kevin was still alive, although barely, was a concern to them. They had expected him to have died by now. He was obviously stronger than he looked. It would only be a matter of days now, they felt sure of that.

"We should have just killed him anyway," whispered the man with the ring.

"But he isn't the one! I told you that! They've caught him on the mainland. It's one thing to get revenge for what he's done but to kill someone innocent.....that makes us just as bad." His accomplice was nervous, constantly looking around him all the while, even though the island was isolated at this time of year.

"Well, he shouldn't have tried to escape. If he'd just waited, we may have let him go. There's no way that we could release him after he injured himself. He's seen us now and he knows what we both look like. If we let him go now, it will only be a matter of time before the police come after both of us." He made a point of stressing that they were both in this together.

"So, we just leave him here to die?"

Ring man nodded, "Hardly anyone comes here at this time of year. By the time they do, he will be unrecognisable and it will be impossible to pin this on us. It will be just another unsolved crime, besides who cares about him? He's an outsider, of no interest." He checked the padlock to ensure it was securely locked. "Come on, let's get going."

As he picked up his bag from where he had left it lying by the door, the sunlight caught his ring. Its reflection bled through the gaps of the wood and played on Kevin's face. Kevin took one shallow sigh and then all was silent.

Chapter 25

Karen sat at the nursery window in the rocking chair that they had bought together when she had first found out that she was pregnant. As she rocked back and forth, gently stroking her stomach, she felt a sudden rush of warm air over her face along with the familiar smell of Kevin's aftershave. A solitary tear made its way down her cheek. A sob caught at the back of her throat as she felt certain that Kevin was dead.

Chapter 26

At exactly the same time that Karen knew, without a shadow of a doubt that Kevin was dead, Annie paused from her task of packing her bag. The air had taken on a strong cigar smell and she could feel a solid pressure against her chest. Just as Karen had instinctively known that at that moment Kevin had died, so did Annie.

Carefully folding the aran jumper that she was holding, Annie placed it into her bag and then sat down heavily on the bed. She leant forward and put her head in her hands. All she could think of was Kevin's pregnant wife. What a way to bring a child into the world!

Richard, who had been in the kitchen emptying out Annie's fridge in preparation for her extended stay at Lisa and Dan's house, walked through into Annie's bedroom carefully balancing two mugs of coffee while Bonnie attempted to shove past him to get to Annie. When he saw her sitting with her head in her hands, he immediately jumped to the wrong conclusion that something had happened to Lisa. "Annie?"

She lifted her head and with a half hearted smile and watery eyes she held out her hand for the mug of coffee he was offering her. "Thanks, I could do with this."

"Is everything alright? It's just when I walked in I thought maybe something had happened to Lisa."

She shook her head while blowing on the coffee. "No, it's not Lisa. It's Kevin. He's dead."

"Are you sure?"

Annie nodded as she took a drink from her mug.

"But how are you sure Annie? How can you be so certain?"

She put down her mug and walked over to the window. It was another cold day, the sky heavy again with snow. She smiled as she saw a lone walker out with their dog on the beach. She turned back to look at Richard, all the immediate emotion and upset that she had felt just a few moments ago had gone. She knew what she had to do although she wasn't quite sure how. It was time to find Kevin so that his wife could say her final farewell.

Wrapping her arms around herself, she tried to answer Richard's question as honestly as she could.

"How do I know? In exactly the same way that I know where he is and what he went through. It's all about how I feel, what I see, hear and smell. I know he is dead and I also think that his wife knows as well."

Richard walked over to Annie and without needing to say anything, she moved towards him. He wrapped her in his arms and kissed her with such gentleness that it made her want more.

"You never to cease to amaze me Annie. I never thought that when I came back home for Christmas, that I would end up getting up close and personal with a psychic."

She laughed. "Well, considering I'm sworn off men, it's taken me by surprise."

"Call yourself a psychic? You should have seen this coming!" he teased as he kissed her again.

"With jokes like that, this won't last long," laughed Anne.

"So, this is something then?" he gently quizzed.

She kissed him lightly. "It's something that is in its early stages and that I quite like. Will that do for now?"

"It will do for me. So, what do you need to pack next?"

Annie moved over to her bag and placed the folded jumper into it. "I thought that this would do for now. I want to pop back here every other day anyway. Lisa's house is only a ten minute drive away so it's not exactly necessary to pack everything."

"It gives you an excuse to have a bit of time on your own as well."

She glanced up, "That obvious?"

He shook his head, "Not really, but I can imagine that you will need a bit of time on your own if Lisa is really bad."

She nodded, "I've promised her that I will be strong but sometimes it can be very hard."

He came across and hugged her again. "You'll be fine. You are a lot tougher than you think. Besides, you've got me looking after you now."

She pulled back from him. "Aren't you supposed to be going back to London soon?"

"Well, I've been thinking about that. Being back up here has give me a bit of time to reflect on what I want and what is important and believe it or not, I miss this place."

She smiled, 'Dornoch does have that effect on you doesn't it?" I could not imagine being anywhere else."

"To be fair Annie, I think you and Lisa have both got the best views in the whole of the village so you are bound to be a bit biased!"

"Biased and very lucky," smiled Annie.

"Come on, Bonnie is desperate for a walk and Lisa will think I've smuggled you back to London if we don't get round there soon. Why don't we go for a quick walk on the beach, then head over to Lisa's?"

Annie zipped up her bag, grabbed a jumper and hat from the wardrobe. "Come on Bonnie, you heard the man!"

Richard was already waiting at the back door wrapped up as if he was about to walk out into the North Pole. "Gone soft have you!" teased Annie.

He pulled her hat down over her eyes, "Less of the cheek you! It's really cold out there. Aren't you going to put something else on?"

She laughed him off, "Don't be daft! Us highlanders are used to the cold." It did not stop her taking a sharp breath as he opened the door. "Crikey it has got colder. Let's make it a quick walk!"

"And you had the cheek to call me soft," he scolded. The three of them made their way down the garden and out through the gate that led onto the beach. The tide was out and all that was visible were miles of golden sand flecked with snow.

As they walked along the shoreline, a fighter jet flew overhead out on its manoeuvres from the airbase at Lossiemouth. They paused to watch and Richard gently took hold of Annie's hand. She was aware of his warmth even through the thickness of their gloves.

"I love watching the jets fly past. I often come out here with Bonnie when the beach is empty. We sit and have our own personal airshow."

Richard nodded, "It is brilliant isn't it. I never cease to be amazed at the noise they make." Bonnie let out a bark as another jet made its approach.

"Come on you two, it's time we got you both to Lisa's. Do you need to do anything else before we go?"

Annie shook her head, "Nope, ready as I'll ever be."

As they slowly made their way back to the house, Richard took the opportunity to quiz Annie more on her reasons for not contacting the police about Kevin. "Surely it's worth an initial knock-back if it gets your message to his wife?"

"But what if they don't tell her?" countered Annie.

"We try again and again until they do. You said it yourself Annie, his wife needs to bring him home and have the chance to say goodbye properly."

"I know. It's just that I always feel as if I am on trial when the police are involved."

"Well, you have Dan, Lisa and me all behind you, so there is no reason for you to feel as if you are on your own with this."

"Okay, let's get to Lisa's and then we'll give the police a call."

He squeezed her hand, "That's my girl."

Chapter 27

Annie only needed to take one look at Dan's face as he opened the door to know that something was seriously wrong.

"What is it Dan?"

He rubbed his hands over his face, "She's really bad Annie. I know she doesn't want to go into hospital but I think she might have to."

Annie rushed past Dan and ran up the stairs two at a time. She pushed open the bedroom door and was met with the image of Lisa curled up in a ball, writhing in agony. Annie quickly positioned herself on the bed so that she could very gently hold Lisa and stroke her hair. All the while talking gently in an effort to calm her.

"Lisa we need to get you to hospital."

Lisa groaned, shaking her head.

"Come on Lisa, just this once. The pain relief obviously isn't working. Let's just get it sorted and then we'll bring you home."

"If I go in, I'll never come out!" sobbed Lisa.

"Don't be silly. Please Lisa, for me." Annie turned towards the bedroom door and was met with two worried faces. All the colour had drained from Dan's face and Richard had an arm around his shoulders, trying to reassure him.

Dan cleared his throat, "I called the doctor just before you arrived. He shouldn't be any more than five minutes." Annie smiled reassuringly at Dan. "Knowing Gordon, it will be more like two minutes!"

As well as being the local doctor, Gordon was a close friend. He had been with Lisa every step of the way, from her initial diagnosis, all the way through her treatments and then to finally agreeing to her wish to be left to die with dignity when the time came. It was thanks to him and the many strings that he could pull that had allowed Lisa to have a large amount of her care at home since the return of her cancer.

"Hello!" Gordon called up as he made his way into the house.

"Up here!" called back Dan.

Gordon and his wife Rhona joined the men on the landing. Rhona was the sister at the local hospital so it made sense that she had come with Gordon, plus her fondness for Lisa would hopefully help to calm her down. Annie crawled off the bed to let Gordon and Rhona take over.

"Don't make me go into hospital," moaned Lisa. Gordon stroked the hair from Lisa's forehead, noting at the same time that her temperature had escalated alarmingly since Dan had called. "I'm not making any promises Lisa. Let's just see what we can do to get this pain under control," he carried on stroking her forehead while quietly instructing Rhona on what he needed. They worked well as a team and swiftly and confidently, pain relief was administered to Lisa while all the time keeping an air of calm around the group.

Annie took hold of Dan's hand and gave it a reassuring squeeze. His face spoke of the terror he felt at seeing Lisa in such distress.

"Alright Lisa, you should start to feel less pain soon. Rhona, can you give the hospital a call. I need to get Lisa admitted as soon as possible."

A choked sob came from Dan. Annie gripped his hand tighter while hearing Lisa sob louder at the mention of hospital.

"Lisa listen to me. I know that I have promised to keep you away from hospital as much as I can but this is non negotiable. Your temperature is off the scale and we need to work on your pain relief. Two days tops, I promise you." Gordon glanced up at Dan, "Have you got a bag ready?"

Dan nodded, "It's in the spare room."

"I'll get it," offered Annie, "You stay here."

As if on automatic pilot, Annie walked through to the spare bedroom to collect Lisa's overnight bag. She could hear Rhona downstairs finishing off her call to the hospital. Fragments of the conversation drifted up, each word making Annie shudder.

"Terminal..........."

"Serious condition........."

Annie closed the bedroom door in an attempt to block out the words. Leaning against the door she counted very slowly to ten and took a deep breath, shaking her head as if trying to wipe away the image of Lisa in pain. Composing herself, she picked up the overnight bag and made her way back along the landing, to the main bedroom. She could see that Lisa's body had relaxed and that Dan was now sitting beside her, talking quietly about light hearted moments in an attempt to divert her attention away from all that was happening around her.

Richard took the bag from Annie. "You okay?"

She nodded, unsure if she could speak.

"Gordon says that what he has given her will knock her out for a few hours. Once he gets her to hospital, he'll be a lot happier."

"Ambulance is here!" called up Rhona.

"I'll carry her down Gordon," Dan rose from the bed.

"Well, it's against regulations mate, but I'm not going to stop you."

Dan lifted Lisa from the bed and gently carried her down the stairs to the waiting ambulance.

Richard followed behind Dan. "I'll bring Annie to the hospital in the car, do you need us to bring anything?"

Dan shook his head, "No thanks mate, just lock up before you come."

The ambulance men helped Dan in. "Hey Lisa, do you want the full works tonight or a silent arrival?" joked one of them.

This was one of the benefits of living in such a small town as Dornoch. Everyone knew each other and Lisa had earned much love and respect from the villagers over the years. As the ambulance drove away, Gordon turned to Annie. "You know the drill by now. I'll see you down there. Don't worry Annie, we'll get it under control."

Annie nodded, "Thanks Gordon. I honestly don't know what we would do without you."

Rhona walked over and gave Annie a hug. "It's hard I know but Lisa is very lucky to have you and Dan. Not everyone is as fortunate."

"Right everyone, to the hospital!" called Gordon.

"We'll follow in a few minutes, we just need to lock up."
Gordon and Rhona waved goodbye and then headed off,
following the silent blue flashing light a few hundred
yards ahead of them.

"Come here you." Richard held out his arms and Annie
walked into the comfort of his embrace, holding on for
dear life. "I'm here for you now and I am not going to let
you go through this on your own." She nodded into his
chest. "Right, let's get the house locked up. Bonnie, you
can be guard dog!" Bonnie thumped her tail and sat by the
back door. "Annie, is there anything else we need to
take?"
"No, I've got everything."

As they made their way to the hospital, Richard laid a
hand on Annie's knee. "Has she ever been as bad as
this?"
Annie shook her head, "Never as bad and never as
quickly."
"Scary stuff."

"I know. Thanks for helping. You've really jumped into the deep-end with us haven't you?"

He smiled, "That's what friends are for. Let's just hope that Dan is okay. He looked as if he was about to collapse."

They made the rest of their journey in silence, both lost in their own thoughts at how dreadful the scene had been when they had arrived at Lisa and Dan's.

The glare of the hospital lights met them as they turned the corner. "Park here. They normally admit Lisa into the ward over there," pointed Annie.

Walking down the hospital corridor hand in hand, Annie could see Dan and Gordon up ahead. Both men played for the local rugby team and it always made Annie smile that such hulking, big men, could be so soft when it came to Lisa.

"How is she?" Annie looked up at Gordon.

"She'll be fine. We all knew that these episodes would get worse. We just need to get the medication under control and work out how we can give her what she needs."

Gordon paused, clearing his throat before saying more.

"This is really hard for us all. Lisa is a very special person and I will do everything I can."

"There's a huge 'but' there Gordon. Come on, we always promised total honesty." Dan's face was composed but Annie knew that just below the surface he would be frantic.

Gordon shifted uneasily, "Let's get Lisa settled tonight and we can discuss this tomorrow."

Dan shook his head, "Come on Gordon, out with it!"

Gordon looked from Dan to Annie. He was obviously torn between his friendship and professionalism, he sighed heavily. "Well, as your doctor and your friend, you need to start preparing yourself for a hard time ahead. Lisa's latest results have come back and the cancer is much more aggressive than we had hoped. It's hard to say without carrying out a few more tests but at this stage we are looking at weeks rather than months.

Dan physically staggered backwards. At the same time Annie felt as if the room was swimming in front of her.

"Sit down, both of you!" ordered Gordon. "I know that this isn't the right place to tell you something like this but we've known each other too long."

"It's fine Gordon. I appreciate the honesty. It's just a lot to take in." Dan shook his head, "I'd just really hoped that we would have longer but I think we both knew."

Annie reached over to hold his hand. "We're all in this together Dan. We'll do everything we can to make the time left as comfortable and happy as possible for Lisa."

He squeezed her hand, "You can't break up our gang without a fight."

Annie nodded, "Damn right!"

Rhona popped her head around the door of Lisa's room. "She's asking for you both."

"Ready?" Dan stood up still holding Annie's hand.

"Always," she replied.

Walking into the dimly lit hospital room, Lisa looked so serene lying in bed.

"She's obviously heavily sedated but I didn't dare make her wait any longer for you both to come in," whispered Rhona. Annie and Dan smiled.

164

"I'll leave you to it, just press the button if you need anything. Gordon and I will stay for a couple of hours just to make sure that Lisa's temperature stabilises.

"Thanks Rhona. We can't thank you and Gordon enough." Dan hugged Rhona before moving over to Lisa's bed.

"Making moves on the nurses now are we?" mumbled Lisa.

Dan laughed. "Can't get anything past you can I? Get some sleep. Annie and I are here and we're not going anywhere."

They sat on either side of the bed, each holding Lisa's hand. Richard opened the door quietly and stood just at the entrance. "Do either of you want a coffee?"

"Yes please," they whispered. Richard nodded and headed back out down the corridor on the hunt for a vending machine.

Dan looked across at Annie, "You okay?"

"I'm fine. What about you?"

"Shaken not stirred is probably the best description."

"Fool!"

The rest of the night was thankfully uneventful. Rhona and Gordon carried out regular checks on Lisa while Richard played the role of tea boy.

As the sun came up on another cold, frosty morning, Lisa slowly opened her eyes. Looking around her, she could see that Annie and Dan had both fallen asleep in chairs positioned on either side of the bed as if they were gatekeepers. Richard was stood staring out of the window.

"Morning," croaked Lisa.

"Hey you." He turned towards her. "How are you feeling?"

"Not bad, considering last night's events." She looked across at the sleeping pair. "What about those two?"

He glanced across at Annie and Dan. "They're fine. You gave them quite a scare you know."

"Come over here Richard. Come sit beside me."

As he sat on her bed, holding her hand, she looked straight into his eyes. "Look after her for me. Please don't hurt her."

"I have no intention of disappearing. She's a tough nut to crack, but I feel as if this is where I belong. I know it sounds soft but I really do feel as if at long last, I have come home to stay." He gave her hand a gentle squeeze, "Do you need anything? Water? A nurse? Gin?"

She squeezed his hand back, "A glass of cold water would be wonderful thanks."

As he made to rise from the bed, Lisa gripped his hand tighter. Richard turned to ask if there was anything else that she needed but could instantly see that she was becoming distressed. "What is it Lisa? Is the pain back?" He leaned over to press the buzzer but she shook her head.

"I'm scared Richard. I've never really said it out loud before but I am really scared now. What if I am made to stay here? I want to go home." Her eyes welled up with tears and Richard knew that she would be fighting hard to stay in control of her emotions. He sat back down on the bed, gently holding her hand, giving her time to compose herself.

"Lisa, you are the strongest person I have ever known. I've known you an awfully long time and you have always been the one person who keeps everyone else on the straight and narrow. I've lost count of the amount of times that you have helped us all out over the years." He gently pushed a stray lock of hair behind her ear. "You are a wonderful, caring person and I guarantee that between the two sleeping beauties and myself that we will make sure that you spend the time left to you in the comfort of your own home, with your friends and family to support you."

"You always were a charmer," she smiled.

"Only to the most beautiful of women," he grinned back at her. "It's good to see a smile back on your face. Let me get you that water and then I'll wake this pair up." He lifted her hand to his lips and gently kissed it. "Don't get up to anything while I'm not here, those two would never forgive me."

Chapter 28

"Mind you don't fall off that chair!" warned Richard. He was watching Annie put the finishing touches to the Welcome Home banner that they had put up for Lisa's return from hospital.

It had been three days since her 'bad turn' as they all now termed it and Gordon had agreed that she could come home today. Dan had headed off to the hospital, promising to bring Lisa back as soon as possible. They had all missed her presence in the house terribly and although neither Annie nor Dan had voiced their feelings out loud, they both knew that this had been a taster of what was to come. Neither of them had felt that they had handled it very well but at least they were getting Lisa home today which was all that mattered to them both.

"Put the kettle on Richard, they'll be back soon."

"Yes, Miss Bossy Boots" he laughed.

"Better get used to it if you're staying for the foreseeable" she joked back at him. As she made to step down from the chair he strode over and grabbed hold of her waist and lifted her down. Kissing the top of her head and hugging her, he whispered, "You okay with what Dan and I have planned?"

She hugged him back, "I won't say that this isn't going a bit faster than I anticipated but I am thrilled to bits. It helps Lisa and Dan out and gives us time together, which I never thought that I would hear myself saying."

"My parents were quite surprised but at the same time thrilled to have the chance to see a bit more of me."

"I can't wait to tell Lisa! Dan thought it would be best to wait until she got home and then we can all tell her together."

"You're like a kid at Christmas at the thought of her coming home," he laughed. "It looks like Dan was a lot faster than we thought, here's his car coming up the drive." They both headed for the door, Bonnie following close behind so as not to miss out on anything that was happening.

Dan parked the car as close to the front door as he could and almost skipped his way around to the passenger door. He gently lifted Lisa out from the car and carried her towards the house.

"Make way! Wide load coming in!" It set them all off laughing especially at the dirty look Lisa threw at him.

"I am not a wide load."

"Whatever you say love," chuckled Dan.

Annie had already lit the fire and laid out pillows and blankets on the large sofa ready for Lisa's arrival. Dan placed her down on the sofa.

"Stay," he ordered. "I'm just going to get your bag from the car."

Annie fussed around Lisa, plumping up pillows, straightening blankets, while Richard looked on amused at the frustrated expression that was forming on Lisa's face.

"Annie, Lisa is about to hit you if you carry on fussing."

Annie looked across at Lisa, who had what she liked to call her 'sucking lemons face'. Glancing across at Richard she could see that he was finding it hard to keep a straight face at the scene unfolding in front of him. She stood up from what she was doing.

"Ok Mrs Sour Puss, if you don't want me fussing around you, what would you like me to do?"

"Well, now that you ask a cup of tea and a catch up on where you are with the missing man case would be good."

Richard moved to the kitchen, "I'll get the kettle on, you two can catch up."

"He seems to be making himself at home," smiled Lisa, "anything you want to tell me?"

"All in good time. First things first, how are you feeling? What did Gordon say this morning?"

Lisa made herself more comfortable on the sofa, "I'm fine, just tired. Gordon's been brilliant as usual. The nurse will be coming in twice a day now to check up on me and we'll just take each day as it comes," she squeezed Annie's hand. "I'm so glad you are here Annie. I wouldn't want Dan going through this on his own. He's so tired, trying to run the business and look after me. I'm worried he'll make himself ill if he carries on."

"There's nowhere else I'd rather be," she leaned over and hugged her friend.

Dan came in with her bags while at the same time Richard came through carrying mugs of tea.

"Nice one mate, I'm parched!" Dan grabbed a mug from Richard and sat down on the arm of the sofa next to Lisa. Looking across at Annie, he took a sip of his tea and then with a wink asked, "Have you told her yet?"

Annie shook her head. "No, I was waiting until we were all here as we agreed."

"I'm impressed. I thought you would have spilled the beans by now."

"Will you stop talking as if I'm not in the room please!" scolded Lisa.

Dan laughed. "You can tell the boss is back! So, do we let her in on our latest plan then?" He looked across at Richard and Annie.

"Well, it depends. Maybe we should let her rest first," teased Annie.

"You two are really starting to wind me up now!"

"Okay, okay," laughed Dan. "Richard has had an idea which I think is rather good and means that I can spend all my time with you."

Lisa looked puzzled, "I don't understand!"

Richard spoke up, "I know you're not one for people flowering things up so I'll get straight to the point. Just like I did with these two." He looked across at Annie and Dan who both nodded at him to carry on. "We all know that the time left for you and Dan is precious and the last thing that either of you need is for Dan to be worrying about his business. I've offered to run the company for him until he is ready to come back. My background is the same as Dan's and we used to work together before I left for London so we both know how we work. I've explained the situation to my place and they are happy to work around me as they knew that I wanted some time off anyway for other reasons." He glanced across at Annie. She knew all about the Lucy episode and the fact that Lucy and his best friend both worked for the same company as him. He had already asked his work for a transfer to another office, which they had agreed to but advised would take some time. Annie had promised not to say anything to either Lisa or Dan about it and had kept her promise.

"I don't know what to say," stammered Lisa.

"That makes a change!" laughed Annie and Dan.

"Thank you Richard. From the bottom of my heart, thank you so much. Are you absolutely sure that it's what you want to do?"

"I wouldn't have offered if I wasn't certain. You and Dan need to make the most of your time together. Annie is running the flower shop so that's one less worry for you and if I look after Dan's company then that means the pair of you can relax."

"I think we are very lucky people, love." Dan nodded at Lisa. "Not many people get as great a helping hand as this pair." He raised his mug to Annie and Richard. "We owe you big time."

"So do you have any other announcements to make?" asked Lisa.

"Nope, that's your lot for now," laughed Annie.

"So, what about Kevin? You haven't said anything more about it? How did the phone call with the police go?"

Richard and Dan smirked. "You're in trouble now, you do know that don't you?"

Annie explained to Lisa that she hadn't contacted the police. She explained about knowing that Kevin had died but she just didn't think that the police would listen. Lisa listened, never once interrupting her friend although she was sorely tempted to.

"So, what are you going to do now? You know better than anyone else Annie that you won't be able to live with yourself if you have information that could help his wife."

Annie shrugged her shoulders, "I really don't know. I want to help her but the police are bound to just laugh at me."

"Since when has that ever stopped you before? You know you need to call them, stop stalling Annie, it's not like you. What else is going on?"

Annie looked straight into her friend's amazing blue eyes, "In the past they've asked me to come down and make a statement. This woman lives in Kent, I don't want to go all the way there and leave you."

"Annie, you've got to make the call. I promise I'll still be here when you get back." She gave her friend a reassuring smile. "Come on, you know you have to do it and if you stall then you will regret it."

"I agree," chipped in Dan. "Come on Annie, this is important to us all. Go and ring them."

Annie knew that she would get no peace from any of them so agreed to ring the police later that day, once she came back from the flower shop. There was another wedding order to complete but she had wanted to wait until Lisa was home and settled before heading off to work on the order.

Chapter 29

As Annie and Bonnie walked along Castle Street and past the cathedral on their way to the shop, Annie could not help but reflect on how quickly things were changing around her. Lisa's condition was deteriorating much quicker than either she or Dan were ready for. The arrival of Richard had unlocked emotions which she thought she had kept well at bay. Everything was happening so quickly and she could almost hear the clock ticking away in her head on the countdown of Lisa's time left with them.

It had been reassuring to see Lisa wrapped up snugly on the sofa while Richard and Dan worked through paperwork and orders for Dan's business. For the first time in a long time, she felt that she could breathe a little more easily knowing that there was someone else to help out. She wasn't much use to Dan as far as his business was concerned but at least she could keep Lisa's flower shop open. It had been a lifelong dream of Lisa's to own her own business. She was incredibly artistic and she had such brilliant people skills that it made sense that she should combine the two. Her flower shop had been a dream that had turned into a reality thanks to Dan and she had worked incredibly hard to make sure that it was a success and to make Dan proud of her. What Lisa never seemed to realise was that Dan would have been proud of her whatever she did. His love was unconditional and he was always amazed that someone as special as Lisa was his wife.

Annie smiled remembering their wedding day and how Dan could not take his eyes off of Lisa the whole day. It was almost as if he thought that if he did, then she would disappear in a puff of smoke. Such a perfect match. They brought out the best in each other and their relationship just seemed to go from strength to strength. Annie wasn't sure how other couples would have survived the past few years that Dan and Lisa had undergone. The cancer, the treatment and now the cancer was back. She had heard of some couples who just could not handle the pressure and had split because of it. Not Dan and Lisa. They had become even stronger and most of the time kept positive.

As Annie turned the corner, she could see Sidney stood by the door of the flower shop. She instantly felt guilty, she had completely forgotten that today was his day for visiting Ruby's grave. She broke into a trot, Bonnie following behind her and shouted out, "Sidney! Wait there, I'll be just a second." He waved back to let her know that he had heard.

"Hello there Annie. No need to rush, I've got all the time in the world."

As Annie fiddled with the set of keys trying to find the right one, she apologised, "Sidney, I'm so sorry. I completely forgot today was your day for visiting Ruby. I'll put together something extra special today for you both." As she opened the door she became aware of Ruby's presence just behind Sidney. Today was not the day for solving puzzles however, she would just observe and not ask any questions.

"Not a problem Annie. I heard that Lisa had to go into hospital. How's she doing?"

As Annie turned on the lights she smiled across at Sidney.

"She's ust got home, that's why I'm late. She's not too bad, I'll let her know that you were asking for her."

"She's a good 'un that Lisa. It's not fair that a lass that young should be going through all this."

Annie nodded, "I know. We're just taking each day as it comes and making the best of it."

"Aye, that's the right approach. No regrets eh?"

An odd thing to say, thought Annie. She had a feeling that it must have something to do with Ruby but thought better of asking. "So, the usual yellow roses Sidney?

"Aye lass."

Annie spent the next few minutes putting together a small posy of yellow roses, eucalyptus and asparagus fern while Sidney made a fuss of Bonnie.

"She seems a bit quiet your Bonnie today. Is she coming down with something?"

"I'm not sure Sidney. We're keeping an eye on her and if she's still like that in another few days then I'll take her to see Alistair."

Alistair was the local vet and another friend from school. Annie often wondered why so many of her schoolfriends remained in Dornoch or the surrounding areas. There were only a few who had ventured away, Richard being one of them and even he wanted to come back to stay.

"Oh he's a good lad that Alistair. He'll never be a millionaire that one but he's a great lad."

Annie knew exactly what he meant. Alistair was renowned for not accepting the full fee from those who he knew were strapped for cash. His heart was in the right place but he would never win businessman of the year.

"There you go Sidney. Ruby should like that."

"Lovely, you needn't have gone to all that trouble though."

"My pleasure Sidney. Mind walking up to the cemetery today, it's quite slippy out there."

"I will. Give my love to Dan and Lisa. Oh and I believe Richard is still up here as well?" He had a glint in his eye as he looked across at Annie.

"Have the jungle drums been out already?" laughed Annie.

"Well, Dornoch is a small place Annie. Not much is kept secret round here."

Annie smiled, "Yes you're right, Richard is still here. He's extended his stay so that he can run Dan's business for him for a while."

"That's a great idea. I bet Dan's relieved, he takes on a lot that lad. The pair of them do, that's what makes them such a wonderful couple," Sidney shook his head. "It's an awful thing Annie. There are those that deserve much better and those two certainly do, they've done such a lot for the village."

Annie could feel a knot forming in her chest, she knew Sidney meant well but she just couldn't handle hearing any more. She made her excuses about needing to get on with the wedding order and promised to pass on his best wishes to Lisa and Dan. As she closed the door behind him, she could not help but reflect on what Sidney had said about Lisa and Dan doing so much for the village. They both worked hard for different charities and Dan's business kept quite a few of the locals in employment. They were integral to the village and for the first time

Annie appreciated that this wasn't just her and Dan's loss,

but also the village losing out on someone so special.

With a heavy sigh, Annie got to work on the bouquets

while Bonnie sat by her feet. The cold was making

Annie's fingers stiffen so she popped on a pair of thin

gloves just to keep them mildly warm while she continued

with the arrangements. As she let her mind wander, the

familiar cigar smell wafted across the shop. Annie

continued with her work, wondering what the purpose of

the visit must be this time.

"I know you're here," she called out.

Bonnie lifted her head and looked across to the door.

Annie followed Bonnie's gaze and could just make out a

fuzziness. As she stared, the name Molly came into her

head.

"Are you called Molly?"

The smell became stronger at this and the wind chime by

the door tinkled ever so slightly.   Annie was not quite

sure what approach to take next. Should she just get on

with what she was doing or try to explore more with

Molly? She put down her flowers and looked back across

to the door, letting out a gasp as she did so. Flashes of dark wavy hair and a gentle smile made her take a step backwards and she caught her ankle on the leg of the table. Her legs felt like jelly, she knew who this was but in some way was frightened to ask.

"Kevin, is that you?" The wind-chime tinkled again, even stronger this time. "What do you want?" whispered Annie.

She felt warmth all around her as the presence of Kevin and Molly drew nearer, her hair felt as if it was being gently touched and then a faint breeze by her ear. As she closed her eyes to concentrate on what was happening around her, she heard very faintly 'call the police'. Her eyes snapped open, the air had turned cold again and she could not see anything different. They had gone. Annie turned back to her half-finished flower arrangement. If they wanted her to contact the police then she would but first she needed to finish the order. It would give her time to work out exactly what she was going to say although she needn't have worried. Unknown to Annie, Dan and

Lisa were already in the process of making the call themselves.

Chapter 30

The ring of the doorbell made Karen and Geoff jump.

Looking out of the window, Geoff could see a police car

parked up. He turned to Karen, "Police are here love, do

you want me to get the door?"

Karen shook her head. "It's fine Dad, I could do with

moving about a bit anyway." She struggled out of the

chair. Her bump had grown considerably in the past

couple of weeks which was reassuring but also meant

getting in and out of chairs was proving awkward. Geoff

smiled at her as she passed. He was proud of how well

she was handling things. There had still been no news on

Kevin but Karen had tried her best to remain positive for

the sake of the unborn baby, even after her startling

statement last week that Kevin was dead. She kept telling

Geoff that if she kept positive then the baby would thrive

and be happy.

As Karen made her way to the door, she could see the

familiar figures of Charles and Lucy through the glass.

They had been assigned to Kevin's case and in the short time spent together, the two of them had struck up a rapport with Karen which had made them extra protective over her. They had both been trained to keep their emotions out of any cases that they were involved with but Karen was such a lovely person. Couple that with her being heavily pregnant and you just could not help but become emotionally involved.

"Morning Karen, how are you doing?" Charles smiled at Karen as he and Lucy stepped into the hallway.
"I'm fine thanks. Getting bigger by the hour. Go through, Dad's in the lounge, I'll put the kettle on."

Charles and Lucy took off their coats and hung them over the bannister before making their way through to the lounge. The house was lovely and warm and Lucy could feel her nose thawing out from the biting cold outside. Grabbing a tissue from her pocket, she followed Charles through the hallway into the cosy lounge. She was shocked to see how drawn Geoff had become since they had last seen him just a few days ago. Lucy sat beside him while Charles stood by the fire, warming his hands.

"Hello Geoff, you're looking tired. Are you feeling okay?" Lucy was concerned at the change in him. It was odd how Karen had gone from being distraught in the first few days to then becoming incredibly calm. In comparison to Geoff who now looked tired and haggard.

"I'm fine thanks Lucy, just tired." Geoff shifted in his seat to make room for her.

"Karen looks like she is coping well," commented Charles turning from the fire to face them both.

Geoff shook his head, "I just don't understand it. I know she is upset and I can hear her crying when she goes to bed but the majority of the time she is calm. It's ever since that day when she said she knew he was dead. I keep telling her that there is still hope. After all, no news is good news but she remains convinced that he's gone. I'm at a loss as to what to do. Surely she should think positively rather than assuming he's dead?"

Lucy took hold of his hand. "Maybe it's just Karen's way of handling the situation. We've seen so many people deal with situations like this in a variety of ways. All we can do is carry on with the investigation and make sure that we are there for Karen whatever the outcome." She looked up at Charles, "Why don't you help Karen through with the tea and then we can all have a chat."

Walking into the kitchen, Charles could see Karen standing quite still, gazing out of the window. He didn't want to frighten her as she was obviously unaware of him walking into the room so he coughed lightly before speaking.

"See anything interesting?"

Karen jumped, "Sorry Charles, I'd got a bit lost in my own thoughts there. Tea's ready."

He took the tray from her and they both made their way back through to the lounge. Lucy cleared a space on the coffee table for Charles to lay down the tray while Karen did her best to try and get into the chair as gracefully as she could. Lucy blew her nose, the warmth of the fire was making her nose run even more and Karen smiled at her.

"Catching a cold Lucy?"

Lucy sat back in the sofa, "More a case of thawing out I think Karen!" They all laughed as she blew her nose yet again and Geoff handed her a box of tissues.

"Think you would be better holding on to these!"

"Have a hot drink Lucy, that should help," laughed Karen.

Once they were all settled Lucy cleared her throat, it was one of her nervous 'tells' before she would start to speak about something awkward, Charles noted. He looked across at her encouragingly as he knew she wasn't quite sure how to broach the subject that they had come to talk to Karen and Geoff about.

Karen broke the ice, "Lucy, you've obviously got something you want to ask or say so why not just get it out in the open."

Lucy blushed slightly, "Well, there is something that we want to talk to you about. I just don't want you to be offended or upset, that's all."

"Well, you've got my undivided attention now. Is it news on Kevin? Have they found his body?"

Geoff shook his head, "Love, you don't know he's dead. He could be alive for all we know and probably is."

Karen looked straight at him. "Dad, I know he's gone. Don't ask me how but I just know. All I want is for his body to be found so that I can say goodbye properly." A sob caught the back of her throat as she finished her sentence but she shook her head at Lucy as she made to stand up and come across. "I'm fine Lucy, please stay where you are." She paused to control herself. "So, what is it that you and Charles have come to tell us?"

"Well, as you can imagine in cases like this we get all sorts of weirdos who come creeping out of the woodwork with their own thoughts on what has happened. Personally I think it's shocking how some of these people can think that we would even consider what they call with." Charles shook his head as he spoke. "I've been in the force many years and as long as I have had to deal with missing people cases, there are always the crackpots who want their five minutes of fame stating that they know where the missing person is. Remember the Madeleine

McCann case? It was disgusting what went on there with so called psychics stating they knew where that little girl was."

Lucy broke in, "Regardless of how Charles or I may feel about things like this, we are obliged to inform you of any information that may come our way. We've had numerous calls from local psychics and mediums who say they know where Kevin is and we can show you the details if you like."

Geoff shook his head vigorously, "I don't think so Lucy. I appreciate the fact that you need to advise us of any new information that comes your way but we don't need to listen to any crazy talk!"

"I agree with you in the main Geoff, however we have had one call today that has made us slightly curious. Karen do you want me to go on?"

Karen nodded. "Let's hear what you have to say."

Geoff slumped back in his chair. "This is stupid!"

"Dad, if you don't want to listen then I suggest you leave. I want to hear what Lucy and Charles have to say."

There was an awkward silence as Geoff rose and walked out of the room. Charles and Lucy glanced at each other before Charles spoke up, "Like we said, we do need to tell you of any information we receive. Lucy has all the details so I will let her explain this to you."

Lucy pulled out the relevant paperwork from her briefcase. "If at anytime you want me to stop then I will. I can always leave these copies with you if you would rather read them later."

"It's okay Lucy. I'd rather hear it now if that's alright with the two of you?"

"Well, we have had quite a few calls with the majority of them picking up on the fact that you said in the tv appeal that he was in Malta. To be honest, it only needs someone with a map of the area to start naming places and convince themselves at the same time that they know exactly where he is."

"You said that there was one call that stood out from the rest?" prompted Karen.

"Yes," nodded Lucy. "Ironically the call was made by a friend of the psychic rather than the psychic herself. The difference here though is that they mentioned Gozo. Now we know that Kevin went there for a couple of days break and we have definitely not mentioned that in any of the briefs we have given to the press."

"What else have they said?"

"It's more like a shopping list of information rather than in-depth detail. Certain place names are mentioned. A description of Kevin that ties in with the photo that you used at the press conference. Odd bits n' bobs about a lady who smoked cigars and had a missing tip of her finger. Goodness knows why that was mentioned!"

Karen let out a gasp, "What did you just say?"

Lucy looked puzzled. "Do you mean the place names?"

"No, after that!"

Lucy checked down the list. "Oh you mean the bit about the cigar smoking lady and that she had a missing tip of her finger. Honestly what some people will say!"

Karen shook her head, her eyes brimming with tears, "No-one could know that could they? It's never been mentioned in any reports has it?"

Lucy didn't understand. "What do you mean Karen?"

Karen picked up a photo of her mother that stood on the table beside her. "This is my mother Molly. She died seven years ago. She used to smoke cigars. Not all the time but she did smoke those small, slim ones. She also lost the tip of her right index finger in an accident."

The three of them looked at one another and then Karen broke the silence, "I'd like to speak to this psychic."

"Are you sure Karen? It may well be down to someone carrying out research on you and your family," said Charles.

"How many of your other psychics mentioned a cigar smoking female with a missing tip of her finger?" challenged Karen.

Charles and Lucy both shrugged their shoulders, "None."

"So, as I said before, I would like to talk to this psychic."

Lucy handed over the paperwork containing the details of the call that Lisa and Dan had made. "Alright, I'll give you the telephone number. Do you want me here when you call them?"

Karen shook her head. "No thank you, I'll be fine on my own."

As Karen closed the door behind the retreating figures of Lucy and Charles, she felt for the first time since Kevin's disappearance that they would find his body. All she needed to do now was contact this psychic and find out more about what they knew.

"Thanks Mum," she whispered.

Chapter 31

The walk home from the shop was cold. Annie and Bonnie walked at a fast pace, both looking forward to getting in front of the fire.

As Annie stamped her boots clear of snow at the back door of Lisa's house, she took a look out across the shoreline. The sky was clear of clouds and the stars were out in their thousands tonight. As spectacular as the view was, she was desperate to get inside and Bonnie was giving her the typical big sad-eyed look.

Opening the door into the kitchen, the warmth hit her along with the inviting smell of a curry that Richard was busy working on. She kicked off her boots and padded across the floor to where Richard was standing.

"I didn't know that you could cook."

"There's no end to my talents, you just need to pay attention," Richard smiled at her. He put a hand to her cheek, "You are absolutely frozen! Lisa is through in the lounge, go and join her and I'll bring you both a hot drink in a minute."

"Where's Dan?" asked Annie as she ran her hands under the hot tap in an effort to warm them. She turned to look at Richard who raised the now familiar eyebrow expression.

"In hiding I would have thought."

"Why?" Annie was looking puzzled now.

"I'll leave that for Lisa and Dan to explain. Let's just say that you are not going to be a happy bunny!" Richard carried on stirring the curry. Annie could see that she wasn't going to get any more out of him so made her way through to see if Lisa could enlighten her.

As usual, Bonnie had made her way through ahead of Annie, straight for her position on the rug in front of the fire.

Lisa looked round as Annie came in. "I thought I could hear your voice. Everything go okay with the order?"

Annie nodded, "No problems. We need to get some more stock in but we have enough for a couple of days. I'll ring and organise a delivery tomorrow."

As she flopped down in the chair opposite Lisa warming her numb toes in front of the fire, she noticed that her wallpaper notes had gone.

"See you've taken down the notes."

"Dan has got them and is updating your original list on the computer."

"He doesn't need to do that Lisa. I can do that later, there's no rush."

Lisa lowered her head and fiddled with the tassles, on the tartan rug covering her legs.

"Actually there is," she mumbled.

"What do you mean? What have you done Lisa?"

Richard came through holding a tray of hot drinks. On hearing Annie question Lisa, he did a quick turnaround and walked back into the kitchen which did not go unnoticed by Annie.

"So, what's going on Lisa?"

Lisa looked across at her friend. She knew that she had overstepped the mark but she was hoping Annie would be in a forgiving mood. "Well, you know how you said that you would ring the police when you got back?"

"Mmmm....." by now Annie had her arms folded and was not looking happy.

"Well, Dan and I thought that we might as well do it for you. Save some time and get the ball rolling so to speak."

"You did what!"

"Oh come on Annie. You were going to ring them anyway. What difference does it make if we did it?"

"It's a heck of a difference. I said that I would do it in my own time. How could you Lisa?"

Richard had been listening in from the kitchen. On hearing the raised voices, he thought it best to intervene. "Come on now Annie, there's no point in having a go at Lisa. She thought she was doing the right thing."

Annie stood up, pacing the floor, "But I said that I would do it. Don't you trust me to keep my word?"

"Annie of course we do," reassured Lisa, "but as we all know, time is against us here in a number of ways. I want to know that you have moved this on and hopefully got closure before things get too hairy here."

Annie sat back down. "I'm not happy Lisa."

"Yes, I think we can all see that!" quipped Richard.

"Look Annie, I'm really sorry but I want my friend to be here with me in a few weeks time. I thought that if you could get this sorted out now, then we can all be together when I get worse."

Annie instantly felt regret at having raised her voice at her best friend. "Alright, you're off the hook............for now."

"So don't you want to know what happened?" asked Richard.

"I have a feeling that you are going to tell me even if I didn't want to know."

Just at that moment, Dan came through from his study. Taking in the glum looks from the three of them he guessed that Lisa must have told Annie about the phone call.

"So, everyone happy in here then?" he joked.

"Well, let's just say that the temperature has dropped to chilly!" laughed Richard.

Dan sat on the arm of the chair next to Annie. "We only did what we thought was best Annie. Please don't be cross with any of us. You know you mean the world to us all and if I'm being honest, I was being selfish."

Annie looked at him with a puzzled expression, "What do you mean?"

"Well, I or should I say we, need you here with us. If the police need you to do anything with them then I would rather it was now than in a few weeks time."

She took hold of his hand, "I know. Lisa said the same thing. I'm sorry for getting cross it's just that I felt as if you didn't trust me to make the call."

"Well, you have been stalling!" smiled Dan. "Still friends?"

Annie nodded, "Sorry Lisa."

"I think I deserved it."

"So what did happen when you called?"

Dan moved over to sit by Lisa, placing her legs on his lap so that she could remain laid out. "We gave all the details that you have so far. I offered to email them a copy of the notes as they said that they would advise Kevin's wife of the call. We were advised that there had been several calls from mediums and that they did not usually take any further action apart from informing the family of the missing person."

"Well, at least they have everything we've got over the past couple of weeks. Can't say any fairer than that."

"I did miss out the bit about you thinking he was dead. I thought that the police might get a bit funny with me on that one."

Annie nodded at Dan, "Yes, I probably would have done the same thing."

Richard made to stand up, "Well, there is nothing more for us to do but wait. I'll just finish off the curry and then we can eat. Table or laps?"

"Laps please!" they all chorused.

" Okay, dinner on our knees and a good film it is then!" smiled Richard.

Chapter 32

Karen looked down yet again at the notes that Charles and Lucy had given her earlier that day. The majority of the details were locations and particulars over in Malta but her eye kept being drawn back to the comment about a stocky, middle-aged woman who smoked cigars and had a missing tip of her finger.

Karen shook her head in disbelief. She missed her mum so much. It would be just like her to try to help from the other side. She held the phone in her hand, thinking back to the heated argument that she and her dad had earlier that evening. He was not happy that she was even considering making the call. So much so, that he had gone out for a pint with some friends just so that they could both calm down from the argument that they had earlier.

Karen looked across at the photo of her mum. "Come on mum. Should I ring her? Can't you just give me one little sign?"

Just at that moment the baby kicked, making Karen gasp. She knew in her heart that it was a boy and he seemed to be getting stronger all the time. She sat back in her chair and closed her eyes for a moment. A faint smell of cigar smoke wafted in front of her nose. Opening her eyes quickly, there was nothing to see but she could still faintly smell the cigars.

Taking a deep breath, she picked up the phone and started to dial the number at the top of the first sheet of paper. She crossed her fingers as it started to ring.

Chapter 33

Dan was busy clearing up the dinner plates when he heard the phone ring. "Can someone get that for me please! I have my hands full."

"No problem," called back Richard. Picking up the phone he jokingly answered, "Dan and Lisa's answering service. How can I help you?" Lisa shook her head as she laughed at him. There was a moment's silence on the other end of the phone. "Can I speak to Annie Murdoch please?"

Richard hesitated before replying. He had a feeling that he knew who this was. "May I ask who's calling?"

"It's Karen Lyons here.........Kevin's wife."

Richard glanced anxiously across at Annie, who was sitting on the floor leaning against the sofa beside Bonnie. He wasn't sure how she was going to react as none of them had expected a call back so soon and especially not from Kevin's wife.

"Can you just hold on a second? I'll just see where she is."

Annie immediately looked up. "It's her isn't it?" she whispered.

Richard nodded, "Do you want to take it here or in the study?"

Lisa motioned to Annie, "Annie, take it here. We'll help you out if you start to struggle."

Reaching over for the phone, Annie sat on the sofa beside Lisa before speaking into the receiver.

"Hello, this is Annie."

Karen heard the soft, Scottish lilt to Annie's voice. "Hello Annie. I wondered where the area code was for. Judging by your accent I'd say it's somewhere in Scotland."

Annie laughed gently, "Yes, Dornoch in the Highlands of Scotland to be accurate. Quite a distance from Kent."

"Annie, I had a visit from the police today. They provided me with your notes that your friend emailed across to them. Would now be a good time to talk to you about Kevin and the information that you have given the police? I would really like to understand more about what you have been given so far and if at all possible how and perhaps who gave it to you as some of the information that you have given is quite personal to me."

Annie took a deep breath before speaking. "I can tell you what I have so far but first you need to understand something."

There was a pause before Karen spoke. "Go on."

"I only say what I get. I do not flower anything up or make things up just so that someone likes what they hear."

"I have no problem with that," replied Karen. " I tend to be known for my own straight to the point approach so that works well for me."

"Are you absolutely sure? I know that you are pregnant and the last thing that I want to do is upset you in any way."

Karen reassured Annie that she was fine and that she did not feel that anything else could upset her as much as losing Kevin.

Annie picked up on this last comment. "When you say losing Kevin, have you already assumed that he has passed over?"

Karen instantly responded, "Yes."

Annie sighed. "Well at least we have that out of the way.
I wasn't sure how to tell you that I felt he has passed but
on the other hand, I have felt over the past couple of days
that you already knew that yourself." Annie looked across
at Lisa who gave her an encouraging nod.

"Karen, do you mind me asking who Molly is?"
A sob was all that could be heard from the other end of
the phone. This was exactly the confirmation that Karen
needed. It did not matter what anyone else thought or felt
about psychics. She had the evidence she needed now and
just listening to the gentle voice of Annie made her feel
comforted in some strange way.

Annie panicked at the silence. "Karen........are you alright.
Have I upset you?"

"I'm fine. Molly was my mum. She is the stocky, cigar
smoking lady that you mention in your information."

Karen paused before posing the question that she really
wanted an answer to. "Have you seen Kevin?"

Annie smiled. "Yes I have, only today as it happens. Now
I need to tell you that I am not the type of psychic

medium that sees full-blown apparitions, for want of a better word. Mind you, your mother has taken me by surprise in how strong she has been in making her presence felt! I only saw a glimpse of Kevin but he was there with your mother."

In spite of the fact that they were talking about her dead mother and husband, Karen laughed. "That sounds like mum. She was not known for being a shrinking violet. I think I get my short temper from her!"

They spent the next half hour talking over how Annie had received the information and how Lisa, Dan and Richard had helped her piece the puzzle together.

"That leaves only one final piece of the puzzle then doesn't it Annie?"

Annie wasn't sure what Karen meant.

"I need to get Kevin's body back here. Will you help me find him Annie?"

"Well, I'll certainly help as much as I can. If I receive any more messages or visions then I will let you know straight away."

This was not exactly the answer that Karen was after so she decided to try another approach. "I am going to tell the police and Kevin's company that I want to move ahead with the information that you have given me. The police may drag their heels to be honest Annie, as they were quite scathing about people like you!"

That didn't exactly surprise Annie. She had yet to find a police officer that did support her 'type' of person as Karen put it.

"Annie, the company that Kevin works for have assured me that they will do everything they can to help me find him and have already discussed sending out some people from the UK to Malta, to assist in the search. I want to speak to them about how we proceed from here and then get back to you. Will that be okay with you?"

Annie assured Karen that she was fine with that although she had a nagging worry that Karen was hinting heavily at becoming a lot more involved than just a few phone calls. After exchanging details, Annie hung up the phone and looked at the three expectant faces staring back at her.

Dan was first to speak. "Well? The anticipation is killing me!"

Lisa gave Annie's hand a squeeze, "You handled that really well Annie, I know that it can't have been easy for you." Annie smiled back at her friend, she was looking tired tonight. She hoped for Lisa's sake that she had a restful night as it was taking its toll on her. Looking around at them all she shook her head.

"It wasn't too bad really and to be honest, there's not a lot more I can tell you. You heard the majority of the conversation. The police have given her all the details that Dan emailed across earlier and it was more just a case of going over certain parts of it with her. Molly is her mum by the way."

Lisa frowned. "What's up? Why do I get the feeling that you are holding back on something?"

Annie shrugged her shoulders. "It's not a case of not telling you something. It's more a case of I'm not sure what will happen next. Karen seemed to think that the police were not that interested in what I had to say which unfortunately we already know from past experience is

213

quite normal. She did mention that the company Kevin works for have said that they will do everything they can to help."

"So what's wrong with that?" quizzed Dan. "If they are willing to help then surely that can only be a good thing."

"Honestly Dan, sometimes you can be really thick!" laughed Lisa.

Annie could not help but smile at Dan's innocent comment. "It means Dan, that if this company have said that they will do everything they can to help, then it more than likely means that they will go over to Malta in an effort to find him with the details that I have given."

"Well that's brilliant news!" chipped in Richard.

Annie and Lisa looked at each other, Lisa silently acknowledging what the outcome would be. She voiced her thoughts out loud so that the boys would understand why Annie was concerned.

"You think they'll ask you to go out there as well don't you?"

Annie nodded, "My gut-instinct says yes. We were worried about me having to go to Kent but I think they will want me to go to Malta. It's just a hunch."

"Well, what do we do?" Dan sounded panicky.

"Let's just cross that bridge when we get to it. At the end of the day you and Lisa come first. I think that I would be of just as much use at the other end of a phone once they got there. That is if they do go."

"Well, whatever happens, we'll support you all the way. After all, Dan and I were the ones that started the ball rolling on this one and contacted the police."

Dan held up his hands in defeat. "Guilty as charged!"

Chapter 34

While Annie, Lisa, Dan and Richard discussed what might happen next, Karen was already busy putting the wheels into motion.

She was feeling the most positive she had since this horrible mess had started. She knew her dad would be up in arms when he found out what she was planning but it was her decision. He would just have to believe in her and have faith in what she was proposing.

Her first hurdle would be in persuading Gavin Holland, who was Kevins' boss, about what she wanted to do. She knew that Gavin had a large amount of respect for Kevin and that he was also feeling extremely guilty for pushing Kevin into going over to Malta. Her hope was that he would therefore be willing to help Karen in her proposed plan and if she had to, she would play on his guilt. Anything to get Kevin back.

As she rang Gavin, Karen could not help but wonder at how circumstances can throw such different people together. She was well aware that she had a reputation for being fiery tempered and had caused Kevin an inordinate amount of hurt over the past couple of years. She was never someone who could settle, she was always rushing around, and in a state of high anxiety the majority of the time. What she was very conscious of was that after her conversation with Annie, she now had an overwhelming sense of calm. She had been surprised at how young Annie had sounded. For some reason she had already formed an impression of an elderly woman, not quite what you would see on seaside pier fronts but not dissimilar, however there had been a youthfulness and a caring tone in Annie's voice which had been instantly calming. Then there was Gavin. A man who was practical and to the point. What an interesting meeting it would be to get us all together, she thought.

"Hello, Gavin Holland speaking."

"Hi Gavin, it's Karen here."

There was the slightest of pauses. "Hi Karen, does this mean you have news?"

"Well, not quite. I did have a visit from the police today. More of an update really. I wondered if we could meet up and have a chat about it?"

"I can come round in an hour if you like?"

Karen thought for a moment. "Actually, can I meet you somewhere? I'd rather talk to you about this away from dad."

"Is everything alright? Geoff has been very worried about you."

"Everything is fine, please don't worry about me. In fact, for the first time I feel as if we may be getting closer to finding Kevin."

They chatted for a few more minutes, agreeing on a venue that was close enough for Karen as she was finding that she could only drive short distances as getting behind the wheel was proving difficult due to her ever-growing baby bump.

"Thanks Gavin, I'll see you in an hour."

"Do you need me to bring anything with me?"

"Just an open mind," smiled Karen.

Chapter 35

A gentle tap at the bedroom door roused Annie from her slumber. It had been a late night for them all as they discussed the possibility of Annie having to go over to Malta. Annie had been adamant that she was not going anywhere. As Richard had left to head back to his parents' house for the night, he had held her tightly. The temptation to ask him to stay over had been strong but she did not feel ready yet for that leap in their relationship. Or rather her head told her she wasn't ready yet!

"Annie, are you decent?"

"Absolutely stark naked!" she joked.

"Excellent," was the response from Dan.

He walked into her room carrying a mug of tea and handed it over to her. "Morning sleeping beauty! It's time you were getting up."

Annie glanced across at the clock - 9am. "Crikey Dan, I should be at the shop, placing that order."

"Don't worry about it. Lisa and I thought you deserved a lie-in."

"Still feeling guilty then?" she questioned, looking at him over the top of her mug.

He shrugged his shoulders, "Maybe a little bit."

She moved her legs so that Dan could sit down on the end of the bed. "Are you going into the office with Richard today?"

"No, he's happy to head in on his own. I'll pop in at lunchtime to check on how he's doing. I have to say Annie, it's such a relief that I can hand all this over to him. He's about the only person I trust enough to hand over the reins to."

She blew on her hot tea. "Yes, I have to say, I'm quite pleased myself that he's staying here for a bit."

Dan burst out laughing. "Oh my god! You're really taken with him aren't you? The ice-maiden has finally melted!"

"Less of the ice-maiden you! I would prefer to think that I was more interesting and aloof rather than frosty."

"Whatever you say Annie," laughed Dan.

The doorbell rang. "That'll be the nurse. I'll leave you to get ready. By the way, I think it's time to take Bonnie to see Alistair. She's still quite lethargic and I can't get her to budge from the fire at all."

Annie nodded, "I'll give him a ring and see if I can get her an appointment for later today."

The doorbell rang again. "Good god, how impatient is this woman!" joked Dan.

Annie sat back in her bed and looked out at the view. The snow had finally stopped but the sky was completely white, a sign that it was ready to drop a fresh fall of snow at any moment. She closed her eyes and was shocked to see the face of Kevin. His presence was getting stronger by the day so keeping her eyes closed, she let him lead her to whatever it was that he wanted her to see.

The now familiar landscape from her earlier visions appeared. The bluest of water. A small red and white boat. He then led her up the cliff path and steps. She felt as if she was physically there, walking just a few steps behind him. The landscape around her was quite empty. No buildings, no people, just grassland on either side. As she followed, she took note of a crossroads in the path that they were on. On the left, it seemed to lead to another coastal path. Straight ahead took you to what appeared to be a large building. Annie could not be sure from the distance they were but it looked like a hotel. To the right, the path led uphill to an area which was populated with a variety of trees and bushes.

Kevin pointed to this path and so in her mind, Annie followed. The path was rough, sandy and stony. There appeared to be no inhabitants on the island that she could see. As they reached the top of the hill, Annie was surprised to see that in the small valley below, there was what appeared to be a number of small, well kept allotments. As she walked down the hill, she became aware of her heart beating faster a feeling of agitation but she did not understand why.

Kevin stopped walking and turned to her. He then nodded his head in the direction of a small clump of bushes. From where she was standing, she could just see the top of what looked like a shed. Her heart was hammering so loudly in her chest now. She knew she was close to what he wanted her to see but Annie was not sure if she wanted to move forward. Looking anxiously at Kevin, he nodded at her and smiled encouragingly.

Sharp needle-like thorns scraped at her ankles as she moved through the undergrowth to the shed-like building. Kevin was now behind her, almost pushing her forward. A flash of colour teased her from between the branches. She knew exactly where she was now. This had to be the blue outbuilding that she had seen previously. She reached out with her hand to push back the branches obscuring her vision and suddenly felt warm liquid running down her legs.

Panicking, Annie opened her eyes, "Shit!" Her hand which had been holding the mug of tea was outstretched before her and the tea had emptied out onto her lap. Quickly jumping out of bed and stripping off the tea-soaked sheets, Annie felt cross at herself for ending the episode with Kevin so abruptly. On the upside, it confirmed what she had already seen in previous visions. He was definitely on the small island of Comino or 'come in' as she had originally called it.

Another tap at the door, this time it was Rhona. "Annie, can I have a quick word please?"

"Sure, come in," called back Annie. Shrugging on her thick towelling robe, she opened the door wider for Rhona to enter. "Is everything alright? We were expecting one of the nurses, looks like we're getting a special visit." She nodded back, "Yes fine thanks. I just thought it might be useful if you went through the routine with me, regarding Lisa's new meds. Dan has already passed the test so to speak!" she joked.

"Of course," Annie nodded her head. "Do you want me to come through to Lisas's room?"

"No, it's fine. We can talk it through here plus it gives me a chance to check that you are feeling okay about everything."

"Ah, I see." Annie smiled knowingly back at Rhona. "What you really mean is, you want to check that Dan and I are coping? I know we didn't exactly handle things in a totally confident manner the other night but we did learn a valuable lesson."

Rhona came over and sat on the edge of the bed next to where Annie was standing. "Annie, no-one is judging you or Dan. You have both given Lisa a much greater quality of life here at home than many of our other patients are fortunate enough to experience. Gordon and I are just worried about you both. We have mentioned to you in the past about grief counselling, I know it may seem odd being counselled now but it does help prepare you for what is to come. We both wondered if you had done anything about it yet?"

Annie sat down next to Rhona. "We haven't yet. I could give you a hundred and one reasons why we haven't but none of them are really viable. I suppose we have both just been avoiding the inevitable in our own way. I have been pressuring Dan into sitting down with Lisa to agree her funeral arrangements. She wants to have that all out of the way before things become too bad."

Rhona took hold of Annie's hand, "Annie, you and I both know that things are becoming bad now. Don't let Dan put it off. Lisa needs this time just as much as you do. As hard as it is for you and Dan to discuss arrangements like this with someone so close to you both, it needs to be done."

"Message received and understood. Tell Gordon thank you for caring so much. Without both of you I think Dan and I would have really struggled."

"It hurts us too Annie. Gordon has blamed himself so many times. He keeps wondering if he could have spotted the cancer earlier."

Annie gripped Rhona's hand tighter, "That's just nonsense and you know that! He has done everything humanly possible to help Lisa and he has nothing to blame himself for. It must be very hard to treat someone who you have known for so long and who is a friend." Rhona wiped away a tear, "Look at me! I'm supposed to be checking that you are coping and I end up crying! We just wish that there was more time for you all. You three have been together for so long that it's hard to imagine you any other way."

"She'll still be here with us in her own way. I know that you and Gordon aren't really into all the spiritual stuff but I guarantee you that Lisa will be keeping an eye on us all and giving us the kick up the backside we need when we aren't doing the right thing!"

Rhona laughed, "You know what, I really like the idea of that." Glancing at her watch she rose to leave. "Any time you need a chat Annie then just give me a call. We're here for you and want to help any way we can."

Annie nodded, "Thanks, you might regret the offer."

Annie stood at the bedroom window and watched as Rhona made her way out of the drive. She leant her head against the cold glass, glad of its coolness against her hot forehead. Dan had the heating on continuous and set at a temperature that could only be described as tropical as Lisa felt cold almost all the time.

She was just beginning to fully realise how lucky they were to have the support network that they had. Richard coming back and helping out had been invaluable to Dan and had also opened up an emotional part of Annie that she had kept locked away for a long time. She wanted more but on the other hand was scared to say anything. How would he feel? Did he really have feelings for her or was it just the emotion of the situation? Only time would

tell. For now she was happy to have him here with her to

help out and be a good companion to Dan. He would need

someone strong when Lisa did finally die and Annie knew

that Richard would be able to handle Dan in a way that

she would be unable to in the first few weeks of Lisa's

passing.

The ringing of the house phone brought her back from her

maudlin thoughts. She knew that Dan was busy helping

Lisa get ready so she made her way out to the hallway to

answer it. Without thinking, she picked up the receiver

and said, "Hello Karen."

"How on earth did you know it was me?"

Annie laughed, "Sorry, it's just one of those funny traits I

have. I bet you have them too. How many times have you

known who was at the door before you answered it?"

Karen thought for a moment. "Probably not as many

times as you have!"

It seemed bizarre to Annie that she and Karen already

seemed to have a familiarity between them after only one

call. Even odder considering the circumstances but Annie had learned a long time ago never to question what 'chance' seemed to put in front of her.

"So, what can I do for you Karen? I didn't expect to hear from you for a few days. Did you manage to contact the person at Kevin's work?"

"Yes, I did actually. I met up with Gavin last night after our telephone conversation." There was a slight pause that Annie suspected was probably due to Karen working out how to politely tell her that Gavin thought that people like Annie were a load of old cobblers.

"So did he tell you not to let me darken your doorstep then?"

Karen laughed. "Well I'll admit that the first hour of our conversation was spent debating the whole psychic and clairvoyant abilities of certain famous television psychics, who have done nothing to endear Gavin to anyone who states that they can communicate with the dead."

Annie nodded her head, "Ah, fair enough. At least you had the courage to give it a try. I'm sorry that it didn't work out."

"Hang on! When did I say that?"

"Well, I just presumed," stuttered Annie.

"You presumed wrong then! Gavin is willing to move this forward and help out. He has asked if we could all meet up to discuss this further. Is there any chance that you could come down here as I don't really want to leave home for obvious reasons?"

Annie sighed, she had known that this was bound to happen and after the conversation that she had just had with Rhona, the last thing she wanted was to leave Lisa. She glanced over her shoulder. Lisa's bedroom door was open.

"Hang on a second Karen, I just want to take this in another room." What she really meant was that she wanted to take the call out of earshot of Lisa!

"Hi, are you still there?"

"Yes I'm here. Is everything okay Annie?"

"I'm going to be completely frank with you Karen. It is very difficult up here at the moment." Annie knew instinctively that she could be open and honest about her reason for not coming down. She explained in detail about Lisa and hoped that Karen would not feel let down by what she had to say. Karen listened intently, never once interrupting.

"Annie, I am so sorry about your friend. I understand completely your reasons. Would it be possible for Gavin to speak to you on the phone instead? At least that way he could have a chat with you and work out how he can move this forward."

It seemed a reasonable suggestion to Annie, so once a time was agreed upon for the call, Annie hung up and walked back into her bedroom to finish stripping off the bed sheets.

It did not take long for Dan to come through. "The boss wants to know how the phone call went!"

Annie shook her head trying not to laugh, "I wondered how long it would take. I'll pop through in five minutes and fill you both in. I just need to tidy up here and get a quick shower."

"Don't leave me with her too long, you know how unbearable she can be when she doesn't know what's going on!" They both laughed but at the same time a look crossed between them as they realised that banter like this would soon be a thing of the past.

"Tell her to be patient," Annie struggled to say the words without her voice breaking with emotion. Dan nodded and headed back towards Lisa's room.

Chapter 36

Annie finally arrived at the shop significantly later than planned. As she had expected, Lisa had wanted to know every minute detail of her conversation with Karen. She had overheard parts of the conversation before Annie had moved from the hallway to her bedroom to continue the call. Annie had enlarged upon what had been talked about but did make a point of omitting the fact that she had advised Karen that she could not come down to Kent to meet up with them both. She knew if she let slip to Lisa that she had been asked to meet with Karen and she had declined that Lisa would have given her a hard time about it. They had gone round and round in circles the night before about the potential of being asked to assist in the investigation and although the rest of them had reluctantly agreed that it seemed the right thing to do, Annie was still not fully on-board with the decision.

Lisa had listened to Annie's explanation of the call and although she had said nothing, Annie knew instinctively that Lisa had guessed what had been asked, and was waiting on an opportune moment to raise the subject. Not something that Annie was looking forward to!

The next few hours were spent placing orders with suppliers and catching up on a mountain of paperwork for the shop. Annie had left Bonnie with Lisa and Dan as she still seemed very lethargic but was starting to miss her furry friend keeping her company. She had rung Alistair before leaving the house this morning and explained Bonnie's condition to him. He had not sounded overly concerned and had suggested that as he had not seen Lisa and Dan for a few weeks that he would pop in on his way home tonight to take a look at Bonnie and catch up with them all.

Annie lay down the paperwork that she had been dealing with, she was finding it incredibly hard to concentrate on anything, her mind just would not settle and she felt out of sorts. She knew it was down to the events of this morning, first her abrupt ending to the vision that Kevin had shown her and then the call with Karen. The conversation with Rhona had also brought back into focus the need to work through Lisa's funeral arrangements with Lisa so that Dan and Annie were fully aware of everything that she wanted. It was not something she wanted to do but she had appreciated Rhona's advice that it was something that Lisa would need to feel she had done before things became much worse. She was starting to feel claustrophobic in the shop, she needed fresh air and a chance to clear her head.

Closing up the shop, she headed down to the beach. It had been a while since she had walked alone along the familiar shoreline. As she made her way along Golf Road and passed the clubhouse on her way to the beach, she felt the pressure slowly starting to lift. No one was out playing golf today, but as she passed the clubhouse she could see that it was full of the regulars who did not want to brave the cold wind. She waved at the familiar faces as she passed, then with head bent against the wind and hands shoved deep into her pockets, she carried on along the road, past the Rescue Boat Station and down the slipway onto the beach itself. Whenever she had a problem to solve, she would take herself down to the sea and walk the problem through. The air was sharp and the wind biting but she was starting to feel better. Just being in the wide-open space and having the time to let her mind empty was helping. It was going to have to be a brisk walk rather than a leisurely stroll but either way she knew that this had been what she needed. The jets were flying overhead again carrying out their practice runs. She stopped to watch, letting her mind empty of all the 'noise' of the past few days. Richard had been right. She did need to escape every once in a while when things got too much. She had always known it would be hard as Lisa become weaker but she had not expected to have the additional headache of dealing with a missing person issue.

She became aware of her phone vibrating in her jeans pocket. Fumbling with her gloves, she managed to pull it out. It was a text from Richard. She smiled at the message, 'missing you, see you tonight x'. Here was something else that she had not expected but it was a very welcome surprise. Things happen for a reason, her mum had always said. "You weren't wrong mum," muttered

Annie through numb lips.

Chapter 37

Karen had arranged for Gavin to come round to the house just after five. Her dad was still extremely unhappy that she was still entertaining the idea of becoming further involved with Annie but in fairness, he had acknowledged that if this was what she wanted to do then he would keep quiet about it. If she could get Gavin onboard with the idea of following up on the information that Annie had so far provided then she was hoping that her dad would finally accept that what she was doing was for all the right reasons. She was hoping that once Gavin talked to Annie today that he would be much more convinced, he had made it clear that he was a sceptic. Her dad had told her off, saying that she shouldn't be pinning all her hopes on some psychic mumbo jumbo. In fairness, she was just as taken aback as he was at how convinced she had become that this was the right thing to do. It just felt right and she couldn't really articulate the feeling any better than that.

She could hear the growl of Gavin's Porsche as he approached the house. Her mouth was dry. He had taken some persuading to get this far and she just hoped that he hadn't changed his mind about what they had agreed. Opening the front door, she smiled as she watched Gavin extricate his tall, gangly body from his car. She could not help but laugh out loud at his predicament. Gavin quickly snapped his head up, unaware that he had an audience.

"What's so amusing?"

"You, unfolding yourself out of that car! Honestly Gavin, why don't you just buy a car that suits your height rather than this status symbol?"

"It is not a status symbol!" he retorted.

"Really?" laughed Karen.

He bent back into the car reaching across the driver's seat for his briefcase. The print out that Karen had given him the previous day was in there as well as some quick notes that he himself had made that we wanted to ask this psychic that Karen had become very excited about. Regardless of how convinced Karen now appeared to be, he still needed proof. He had promised that he would do anything he could to help find Kevin, in part due to the fact that he felt responsible for what had happened and

although he may not agree with what he was being asked
to do, he was willing to put his preconceptions to one side
and hear out this woman who believed that she knew
where Kevin was.

Karen closed the door behind him as he made his way
through into the lounge.

"Is Geoff joining us?"

Karen shook her head. "No, he is out in the conservatory.
He knows you're here to speak to Annie but he doesn't
want anything to do with it."

Gavin nodded, he could sympathise with Geoff. He
wasn't exactly sure how he had managed to get himself
into the position where he was going to talk to a psychic
about a work colleague.

"She won't bite you know."

Gavin smiled back at Karen, "Reading my mind were
you?"

She shook her head. "No, but I can imagine how you are
feeling. I was rather tense when I first spoke to Annie but
she puts you at your ease very quickly, it almost feels as if
you are talking to an old friend."

"Well, I will wait until I speak to her myself before I make any judgements." He smiled across at Karen as he started to unpack his briefcase.

They had arranged to call Annie at six. Gavin had come early so that he and Karen could agree a 'strategy' as far as questions were concerned.

"Have you read all the notes that I gave you?" quizzed Karen.

He nodded, "I have, and to be fair to your psychic friend, there are details in the notes that unless you knew the islands well, you would not be able to be as accurate as she has stated. That is presuming that she does not know the islands?"

Karen shook her head. "Both of her friends as well as Annie have all confirmed that they have never been to Malta or even knew about Gozo and Comino."

Gavin fiddled around with his pad and pen. For some bizarre reason, he was starting to feel quite nervous about the upcoming phone call. Karen had been incredibly matter of fact about her dealings with Annie. Anyone who knew Karen well, knew from personal experience that she was a very practical person who called a spade a spade. Gavin himself had been at the receiving end of a couple of verbal barbs from her but she also had a certain way with her that meant you just could not stay angry or offended for long. Impatient was probably an appropriate word to describe Karen. That is what made this whole scenario even stranger. An air of calm and acceptance appeared to have taken over Karen. They had all been startled at her conviction that Kevin was dead. Now there was her conversation with this psychic woman. If nothing else, he could offer an air of common sense to what he felt could turn into a difficult situation if Karen was to accept every word that Annie had said so far.

"Are you ready to make the call?" Karen jolted him out of his thoughts.

"As ready as one can be when about to talk to a psychic about a missing work colleague and friend."

The irony was not lost on Karen. She smiled gently back at him, "You will be fine. I promise."

He nodded. Picking up the phone, he dialled Annie's number.

At the opposite end of the country, an almost identical scenario was being played out in Lisa's house as Annie awaited the call.

Lisa, after much protest, was asleep in bed as her medication was taking its toll on her. Dan and Richard were sat on either side of Annie, trying to boost her morale.

"Just be yourself with this guy Annie. Don't let him be a smart-arse with you. Remember that it's you helping them."

Annie laughed at Dan, he was being very protective about the whole situation. Richard gave her an encouraging wink. Even though they knew that the call was going to be made at an agreed time, when the phone did finally ring, they all jumped.

Casting a quick glance at Richard and Dan, she picked up the phone.

"Hello, Annie?"

"Yes, this is Annie. I presume I am speaking to Gavin?"

"Yes, I've got Karen here with me, along with a copy of the notes that were emailed to her and the police. I thought that as we all know the reasons behind me making this call, we would just get straight to it if that is okay with you?"

Annie nodded. "Yes, I agree. No point in beating about the bush is there?"

Gavin glanced down at his notes. "I would like to understand more about where you feel Kevin is currently located and if possible, try to understand how you received this information."

Annie rolled her eyes. She could tell by the tone of his voice that he was a sceptic and that he was probably only talking to Annie to humour Karen. Knowing this did not anger or upset Annie. She was used to scepticism. What did bother her was that Karen desperately needed closure on this and she hoped for all their sakes that Gavin was not going to be a blocker to it.

They discussed Annie's notes and her feelings on what had occurred for over half an hour. From how Annie had first become aware of there being a problem with Kevin to the conviction of her statement on where he was currently located. She explained how Richard and Dan had helped her in matching the place names from the information that she had received through dreams and visions and the fact that the information that he now had in front of her had been built up almost like a jigsaw puzzle over several weeks.

"I have to be honest with you Annie, I was very sceptical about what I had heard from Karen."

"I can appreciate that Gavin. The good thing is that you have taken the time to listen and understand. That must be a comfort to Karen."

Gavin took a deep breath. "My issue is, that regardless of my initial scepticism, your information is good but I still think that we may have problems with the police over in Malta if we tell them what we plan to do."

"I'm afraid I can't help you with that Gavin. I'm a psychic not a miracle worker!"

Gavin laughed, "Point well made."

Annie could sense that there was something else that he wanted to ask but he was holding back. She smiled to herself as she suddenly saw the name Martha appear in her mind along with a strong smell of cinnamon.

"Gavin, I've just had someone named Martha come through. There is a strong smell of cinnamon accompanying her. Does that make any sense to you?"

There was a long pause before he spoke. She could hear him breathing heavily on the other end of the phone. Clearing his throat, he replied, "Martha was my mum's mum. She literally brought me up as my mum died when I was six." Despite himself, he blurted out, "Does she have anything she wants to say?"

Annie suppressed a giggle, he was not quite the cynic now! Closing her eyes, she could see the words 'I like John'. Rather an odd thing she thought but as usual, she knew to go with the flow.

"I've got the words 'I like John'. I hope that makes sense to you Gavin."

Again another pause. "No-one knows about that Annie. That name you just gave me is someone I met only a couple of weeks ago. I'm sort of hoping that it may lead somewhere if you get my drift."

"I understand," replied Annie. It seemed apparent that he had not discussed his sexuality with Karen.

"Annie, I need to ask you a rather big favour."

She knew what was coming before he asked but rather than help him out, she was trying to stall the inevitable.

"I need to contact the police in Malta about what I plan to do. I obviously want to get over there as soon as I can especially with the information that you have given us. Karen has explained to me about the current situation at home for you and your friends. I realise that it is an incredibly difficult time for you, but is there any way that you would consider coming over to the islands with me to help find Kevin? You have a picture in your head of the exact spot which no matter how hard we try, we won't be able to fully explain to them."

Annie could feel the tears pricking at her eyes. Any other time, she would have agreed to the request but Lisa only had a few weeks left and she wanted to be here with her friend. She felt guilty for not wanting to help Karen in what was a desperate time for her but she needed to stay here, she did not want to lose any of the precious time she had left with Lisa.

"Gavin, any other time I would have said yes but I just can't leave here, you do understand my reasons?"

"I understand Annie," he sounded defeated. "Do you mind if I call you back later?"

"Of course not. As I said to Karen, I'll help out as much as I can."

They spent the next few minutes exchanging mobile numbers as well as discussing his contacts over in Malta.

"Thanks for your help Annie."

"No problem. Just let me know how you get on with the police." Annie replaced the receiver while at the same time rubbing her ear with her free hand. It ached from holding the phone to it for so long.

Richard rose and walked over to the sink. As he filled up the kettle, he turned to the others, "I think we could all do with a brew!"

"Annie?" questioned Dan, "How long would you need to go for?"

"I don't know, anyway it doesn't matter, you heard me say to Gavin that I couldn't go."

"But wouldn't it help them find Kevin quicker if you did?"

Annie shook her head, "I can't answer that Dan."

Richard brought over the mugs of tea. "Are you thinking what I'm thinking Dan?"

Dan took a sip of his tea and nodded. "If you mean that I think Annie should go over for a couple of days, yes."

Annie shook her head vigorously, "I can't do that. I need to be here. Lisa is getting worse, I don't want to leave her."

Dan took hold of Annie's hand. "You would never live with yourself if you didn't go and more importantly, Lisa would be angry with us all."

"But what about the shop?"

"You're grasping at excuses now Annie. Worst case, we can shut the shop for a couple of days. There is always

Denise, she's helped out in the past and she did tell us that she can help out at any time."

"Why not talk to Lisa about it Annie?" suggested Richard. "See what she has to say about it all."

Annie nodded, "I'll have to tell her what went on anyway. It's like the Spanish inquisition with her!"

A knock at the door made them all jump. "It's Alistair,' said Richard looking out of the kitchen window.

"God, I'd totally forgotten that he said he was coming! I'll let him in." Annie jumped off her stool and headed to the front door. It didn't go unnoticed by her that Richard and Dan were talking quietly together, she didn't need to be psychic to guess what that was about!

As she opened the door to let him in, she was reminded at how Alistair's breezy nature always brightened up any room that he walked into. Annie always loved the fact that when she looked at him on the sly to see what colour his aura was, it was constantly full of orange. To Annie, the colour orange meant much energy and he certainly did have a lot of that!

"Evening all! How are you all doing?"

Richard had not seen Alistair for over a year, so they spent the next twenty minutes catching up on news. Dan had gone upstairs to wake up Lisa as he knew that she would not want to miss out on his visit.

"I think it's great that you are helping out Dan. He works far too hard that one! They both do, it will be good for Dan to let go and spend his time with Lisa."

Richard nodded, "I'm just glad that I can help."

"So where's the patient Annie?"

"By the fire, usual place. She's still quite lethargic, I am really starting to worry about her Alistair, what if it's something serious?"

"Well, let's have a look and see what's up with her, I'm sure she is fine but you're right to be cautious."

As they walked through to the lounge, Alistair joked at how the jungle drums were sounding all the way through Dornoch about Annie's love life finally taking an upturn.

"You can really go off folk!" retorted Annie.

"It's only a bit of fun Annie. Anyway, the rumour around the town is that the new man on the scene is not a million miles away from here! Is it true?"

"Oh for goodness sake! Are you not busy enough at the vets that you are now listening to gossip?"

"You're never too busy for a bit of gossip," laughed Alistair. Bonnie lifted her head at the sound of Alistair's voice. "Hello there old girl, got a severe case of laziness have we?"

Annie laughed, "Honestly Alistair, it's just as well you've chosen to be a vet rather than a doctor. Your bedside manner is terrible!"

After checking Bonnie out, Alistair rose from his position on the floor and smiled at Annie, "Well it looks like Bonnie is going to be a mum! I need you to bring her into the surgery and we'll give her a scan but she seems fine."

Annie bent down and gave Bonnie a hug. "Crikey Bonnie, you're a proper grown-up now."

Dan walked into the living room carrying Lisa in his arms. "Evening Alistair. So what's the prognosis?" He placed Lisa gently onto the sofa.

"Well, Bonnie is officially up the duff!"

Dan roared with laughter, "Nice one Bonnie."

"Oh you all think you're very funny, don't you!" Annie sat on the floor gently stroking Bonnie's head. "I think she is a very clever lady."

"Are you going to stay for something to eat Alistair?" asked Lisa. "I heard the boys talking about getting a takeaway. You're more than welcome to join us."

"If you're sure I'm not imposing? That would be great, thanks. I haven't had a chance to catch up with you all in ages. The surgery has been mad busy."

Annie smiled at the scene, it was good to see everyone together chatting and joking. It gave Lisa the air of normality that she constantly craved for. Lisa looked across at Annie, she wanted to hear her version of the phone call with Gavin. Dan had filled her in with the majority of it but she knew that Annie would be feeling confused about what to do. She needed to put her friend's mind at ease but now was not the time with Alistair

staying for dinner.

She gave Annie an encouraging wink, perhaps it was

good to have Alistair here tonight. It would give Annie

the distraction that she needed from her telephone

conversation with Gavin and it gave herself, Dan and

Richard time to work out how they could persuade Annie

to go across to the islands for a couple of days. It had to

be soon though, she could tell that she was getting worse

quickly and her conversation with Gordon had been

honest and frank. He had advised her that best case she

had six weeks left. It was not a long time to ensure that

her best friend and her husband were prepared for the

inevitable. She wanted Annie to have seen this missing

person case through to its end and then she would be able

to stay with Lisa without feeling guilty. It was a big ask of

her best friend but it needed to be done otherwise Lisa

knew that Annie would never be able to move on from the

guilt she would feel at not helping Karen.

Chapter 38

While Annie was enjoying the distractions of a Chinese takeaway and lively conversation, Gavin was busy discussing the latest 'discoveries' as he was now calling it, with one of his contacts in Malta.

The police in Malta had not discounted what he had told them but they were not being overly encouraging. What they were agreed upon was that they had no new leads in Malta itself. After several conversations and a few strings being pulled by Gavin, they had agreed to assist him with a limited resource. Gavin expressed his thanks.

"Will you be bringing the psychic with you?" queried his contact.

"I'm not sure at this stage. There are some complications at home which means she is reluctant to make the trip over."

"Well, let me know what you decide. I'll meet you at the airport and then we can take the helicopter over to Comino."

"That's great. Thanks for all your help. It is greatly appreciated." Gavin put down the phone.

"Well?" Karen's eyes were moist with tears. She was finding the tension hard to deal with. It didn't help that she had just had another heated argument with Geoff. He had been convinced that Gavin would persuade Karen that all this psychic stuff was nonsense. Instead he had seen Gavin actively encourage moving forward with what this psychic had said.

Although Gavin had been in a separate room, he could hear the angry exchange from where he was sitting. He took hold of her hands. "You okay?"

Karen nodded, "I'm fine. I just hate arguing with dad. I know exactly where he is coming from but at the same time, if we have a genuine lead then I think we should follow it. You've spoken to Annie. You agree with me that she is genuine in what she is saying?"

"I can't deny that Annie definitely has something. If she can convince me then she must be doing something right."

"It's not just a case of convincing though is it?" pushed Karen. "She told you something didn't she?"

Gavin nodded, "Yes she did. I'm not prepared to discuss it but yes, she can't have known the information she gave me beforehand."

Karen sat back in her chair, closing her eyes. "I'm so tired. We need to find Kevin."

"We will Karen. I promise you."

"I just wish that I could come with you. Do you think you'll be able to persuade Annie to go with you?"

Gavin shook his head. "At this stage I really don't know. It's obviously an awful time at home for Annie and her friends. I can understand why she is reluctant to go out there. I'm just hoping that if she knows that it is only for a couple of days that she might change her mind."

"I'll keep everything crossed," mumbled Karen, half asleep now in her chair.

"We both will," whispered Gavin.

Chapter 39

Annie walked into the kitchen, to what could only be described as a bombsite. Alistair had not left until the wee small hours and as today was Saturday, there had been full agreement last night that they would all have a lie-in and tidy up late morning.

She let Bonnie out the back door and poured herself a large glass of cold water. The after effects of too much wine were starting to make themselves felt. Bonnie barked to be let back in. As she shut the door on Bonnie's disappearing figure, Richard appeared in the doorway. Annie flushed slightly, which did not go unnoticed by Richard.

He smiled at her blushes, "I can't imagine what you have to be embarrassed about?"
Annie flushed an even deeper red. Richard walked over and held her close. "You okay?"
"Mmm...hum..." mumbled Annie into his chest, "I'm more than okay."

Dan walked in on the two of them. "Oh aye! Decided to stay the night then?" he laughed.

Annie blushed again. Dan winked at Richard, "I'll just get a glass of juice for Lisa and then I'll leave you two lovebirds to it."

As he walked out of the room, he started to whistle the old Van Morrison song 'Have I Told You Lately that I Love You' much to the amusement of Richard.

"Well, we've been officially caught."

Annie smiled, "We won't hear the end of this you know."

"I don't have a problem with that, do you?"

She shook her head, "I'm more than fine with that." She felt happier than she had done in a long time. Richard staying over had made her realise just how much she had missed being with a man. He had been gentle and considerate as well as passionate. Just thinking about last night made her smile.

"Is it too early to say I love you?" he gently asked.

Annie turned her head back into his chest, "I was just thinking the same." At the same moment, her mobile rang. As it vibrated across the worktop, Richard kissed her.

"You better get that."

"Yep."

He kissed her again. "Go on, it could be important."

Annie reached over for her phone. She didn't recognise
the number "Hello?"

"Annie? It's Gavin." Here we go again thought Annie.
She mouthed the word 'Gavin' to let Richard know who
was on the other line. He raised an eyebrow and walked
over to the fridge to pour them both some juice. He was
feeling just as dehydrated as Annie after last night's
alcohol excesses.

"Hi Gavin, what can I do for you?" *As if I don't know*,
she thought.

"I just wanted to update you on the conversation that I
had with the police over in Malta last night. They are very
interested in the information that I passed on from you
and are willing to provide me with an escort to look for
Kevin on Comino."

"That's great news Gavin. How is Karen feeling about it
all?"

"She's obviously relieved that at last we seem to be moving forward but on the other hand, devastated that she can't come with me. The doctor has advised her not to travel, which I have to say I entirely agree with. She is incredibly tired with all that has gone on and although there don't appear to be any problems as far as the baby is concerned, I do worry about what effect the stress of all of this will have on both of them."

Annie sighed, she could imagine exactly how Karen was feeling. She looked across at Richard who was staring intently at her. After Alistair had left last night, they had talked over the feasibility of her flying over to help. Richard, Dan and Lisa were adamant that she should go over for a couple of days but Annie was still not convinced that she should. Any day away from Lisa was a day lost forever and the selfish part of Annie did not see why she should have to help a stranger when she herself was going through an incredibly emotional time.

"Are you still there Annie?"

"Sorry Gavin, yes I'm still here. So, when are you planning on going out there?"

"First thing tomorrow morning."

"Crikey Gavin, that's quick!"

"Well, there is no time like the present and I can't just sit here while nothing is being done over there. We have enough information to at least narrow down the search area and I would never forgive myself if I didn't try." He paused for a second and nervously cleared his throat. I don't suppose you've changed your mind about coming over?"

Annie hesitated before answering. As much as she wanted to be selfish, she knew just as Lisa did, that she would never be able to live with herself. She took another long look across at Richard who seemed to instinctively know in which direction the conversation was heading. He walked over and took hold of her hand, nodding encouragingly.

"If I say yes, there are some provisos."

The sound of relief in Gavin's voice made her realise that she was doing the right thing.

"Annie, we'll do anything you want. It's obviously a very bad time up there for you and I can appreciate that time is something that you don't have a lot of, but I promise you I will do whatever you ask."

Annie was unsurprised to hear that Gavin had already provisionally booked flights for her in the hope that she would come. There were no direct flights from Inverness to Malta so she would have to fly to Manchester and then get a connecting flight to Malta where he would meet her. From there they would then need to be transported across to Gozo. He agreed to ring her back later that day to confirm the exact arrangements.

"I can't thank you enough for this Annie. I know that Karen will feel so much happier knowing that you are coming with me."
"Give her my love and tell her that I will try my best, both for her and her baby."

Annie hung up the phone and laid it gently down on the worktop. The faint scent of cigar smoke was in the air but she knew that Richard would not be able to smell it.
"So, is it action stations then?" asked Richard.

Annie nodded, "Yep. Gavin will ring back later today to confirm the flight times but we fly out tomorrow for two days and then straight back."

"You're doing the right thing Annie. I would rather come with you but we know that's not feasible with me looking after Dan's business, plus I have a feeling I would probably get in the way!"

She laughed at him. "You're probably right but I can't say I'm thrilled at having to go, especially after last night." She blushed again as he roared with laughter.

"Well, you're not leaving until tomorrow. I'm sure we can fit in some extracurricular activity before then!"

Flushing even redder, Annie got up and walked over to the fridge, "Honestly Richard, have you no shame?"

"Not when it comes to you!" he laughed.

She opened the fridge door, relieved of the coolness which she hoped would save her blushes. Her stomach was somersaulting and she knew it was nothing to do with her slight hangover. She had not felt like this for a long time. Even when she was with her ex-husband Ben. Of all the times for her to fall for someone! She never had done anything the easy way.

"What's going on here then?" Lisa had come into the kitchen just as Richard had started laughing. "I hear you didn't go home last night Richard. Was your bed comfy?" Lisa gave him a wink. He burst out laughing again. In spite of everything that was going on, Lisa still had a way of delivering lines in such a deadpan way that you couldn't help but laugh.

"Not bad thanks. I'll just use the shower if that's okay? Annie has something to tell you."

"Oh yes?" Lisa walked slowly over to the fridge where Annie was still standing. "What are you looking for Annie?"

"Nothing" mumbled back Annie. She shut the door and turned to face Lisa, who took one look at her and started chuckling.

"Goodness Annie, have we had a heat wave outside? You're very flushed!"

"Shut up Lisa! It's just the after effects of last night."

"No need to brag!" laughed Lisa.

Annie flushed even redder, "I didn't mean that! You have a filthy mind for a sick person."

"Sorry Annie. What is it you need to tell me? I hope it's not about last night, I love you very much but I don't think I need to know all the details!"

"For goodness sake Lisa, pack it in. You and Dan are acting like a pair of school kids this morning!"

"Okay, okay. I promise not to tease for at least five minutes. What is it you need to tell me?"

Annie took her friend's hands in hers, "Gavin has just rung."

"Ah, I see. Did you do what we agreed?"

Annie nodded, "I've agreed to go for two days only and he is more than happy with that."

Lisa squeezed Annie's hands, "You've done the right thing. I need to see you do this just as much as you need to do it. We've all worked on this puzzle together and I would like to see how it ends." They hugged each other, Annie aware of how thin Lisa was. She could feel Lisa's heart beating against her own chest, her frame had become so frail.

"I will only be gone two days, I promise," she whispered
into her friend's ear.

Lisa nodded and held Annie a little tighter, "Just be
careful."

Chapter 40

The little hut sat on its own amidst the rough track and the wild bushes. Almost as if it was on its own little island. Inside was dark and foul smelling of rotting flesh. In contrast the air outside was fresh and clean, the sun shining brightly down and glinting off the shiny padlock holding its dark secret.

To a passer-by nothing would have appeared out of the ordinary, however if they were to take their time and look closer, they would have seen the faintest of outlines of two figures. One a small, cigar smoking lady and the other, a young, curly haired man. Standing guard. Waiting.

Chapter 41

The silence lay thick between them as Richard drove

Annie to Inverness airport. Occasionally he would glance

across at her and see her shoulders heaving in silent sobs,

tears slowly rolling down her face. Her eyes were red and

swollen with crying. He looked back out at the road

feeling useless. He did not know what he could say to

make her feel any better about leaving Lisa. It had been

heartbreaking to see the two of them as Annie had packed

to leave. He felt guilty at encouraging her to go to Malta

but they had all felt it was the right thing to do. The

problem was, he had not realised how hard it was going to

be for Annie and Lisa to part.

They had already crossed the Dornoch and Cromarty

Bridges and in the distance he could see the Kessock

Bridge that would take them into Inverness. He took

another glance at Annie, her shoulders had steadied now

but he could see that she was just narrowly holding it

together.

"You okay?" he whispered.

She nodded, while blowing her nose, "I'm sorry Richard."

He smiled and with his free hand, caressed her cheek. "I would have been more surprised if you hadn't got all upset although goodness knows what your fellow passengers will think when they see the state of your eyes."

Annie blew her nose again, "Well, I don't care. I'll just wear sunglasses!"

Richard laughed, "They'll think you're someone famous."

She smiled back at him and took hold of his free hand, holding it tightly. A small sob caught the back of her throat and Richard quickly turned to her.

"I'm fine, honestly."

She wasn't though. It had been a very emotional scene back at Lisa's house as they had left for the airport. Everyone had known that this was the right thing to do, but when it had come to the time for leaving, Lisa had become very upset, as had Annie. What she did not know was that an almost identical scene now being played out back at the house as Dan tried to comfort Lisa.

The lights from the airport were now straight ahead of them. Annie took a deep breath, trying to compose herself. As hard as it was for her, she needed to push her emotions to one side and get on with the job ahead. Finding Kevin. She had two days to get to Malta, find his body and then get back to Dornoch. She was determined not to stay a minute longer than was absolutely necessary. There was too much at stake back at home and home was where she wanted and needed to be.

Richard parked the car and turned off the engine. Looking across at Annie, his heart ached. He desperately did not want to let her go on this journey alone. He knew that she was strong but she was also incredibly vulnerable at the same time. She needed people around her who loved her and could take care of her so that she could make the most of her time left with Lisa. Instead he had encouraged her to take this trip and to help find Kevin. He felt guilty but at the same time knew that there was no alternative.

"All set?"

She nodded, her eyes still watery.

He smiled back at her. "It's only two days. It will fly past, you'll see." He was trying hard to be positive but he could feel his anxiety rising. He would not be able to protect her. They both knew his place was here, looking after Dan's business.

"I'll be fine, don't worry," Annie placed her hand gently on Richard's cheek. It felt rough against her hand. He had not shaved since yesterday. She savoured the feeling of roughness against her palm, trying to imprint it into her memory. Something physical to think of when she started her search in Malta.

He placed his hand on top of hers and then turned his face and kissed the palm of her hand. Annie smiled back at him, her stomach somersaulting as it always did when they touched. He leant over and kissed her forehead. "Come on, it's time to get you on that plane."

Annie had deliberately packed light for the trip. She had thrown a few things into a holdall and was taking it on the plane as hand luggage. She wanted to make sure that Gavin realised that when she said two days, she meant two days.

As they walked through the terminal, hand in hand, Annie could feel the tension in Richard. She knew that he was worried about her going on her own. She gave his hand a reassuring squeeze and he turned his head to look at her. She winked at him and he smiled back, holding her hand even tighter.

They slowly approached passport control and the check-in desk in a vain attempt to drag out the few minutes that they knew they had left. Annie handed over her documents while Richard waited off to one side. Her hand felt empty where just a second ago it had been filled with the warmth and strength of his hand. They had left arriving at the airport to the last minute so check-in was about to close.

"Your flights about to be called so you will need to make your way straight through."

Annie smiled back at the attendant, "Thank you." She walked back to Richard. "Apparently my flights about to be called. They've told me that I need to go straight through."

He nodded, "You got everything?"

"Everything I need for two nights," she smiled weakly back.

"Make sure that you are with Gavin or one of the policeman, at all times. For all we know, the men who did this may be watching."

"I'll be fine. Nothing is going to happen. Just straight to the island and then we'll find the area that we have noted down."

He pulled her towards him. "Annie, I'll never forgive myself if something happened to you. It was me that encouraged you to go. I just need to know that you are safe out there."

"I will be, don't worry. We all agreed to this so don't go taking all the blame." She reached up on tiptoe and kissed him.

"Be good while I'm away and look after Lisa and Bonnie for me."

"What about Dan?"

"Oh, he'll be fine, just make sure both ladies get lots of TLC."

He laughed and hugged her hard, "I love you Annie. You come home soon."

"I will," she kissed him again then turned towards the departure gate. Her instinct told her to run straight back into the safety of his arms but the practical side of her knew that she needed to keep her promise to Karen. It did not stop the feeling of foreboding she had. She had kept it to herself but she knew that it was no coincidence that both Richard and Lisa had voiced their concerns.

She turned to wave at Richard as she walked through the gate. He was standing exactly where she had left him. He raised his hand back and winked at her. She smiled back at him, and then walked through the gate, with her head down so that no one could see her tears.

Chapter 42

The flight from Inverness to Manchester had been
uneventful. During the short gap between connecting
flights Annie had used the time to ring home. Lisa was
asleep when she rang, so she chatted to Dan and then
Richard. She felt calmer hearing their voices, reassured
by their words. By the time she boarded the flight to
Malta, she was feeling much more positive. Unfortunately
she was still having problems in shaking off the feeling
that something was not quite right. It was probably just
the upset, she thought, but Annie knew better than that. If
her gut-instinct was warning her about something, then
she would need to stay alert when she arrived at Malta.

She decided to try to take a nap during the flight, in the
hope of seeing some more images from Kevin. As she
slept, she could see the hut in front of her where he had
been hidden. The air was sharp and the sky was the
brightest blue that she had ever seen. The silence around
her was eerie. It was as if all the birds and insects were
holding their breath, waiting on something happening. As

she tentatively walked towards the hut, she could hear her heart thudding loudly in her head. She knew that she should not get any closer. Something was warning her but she felt compelled to keep moving towards her goal. As she slowly reached out her hand towards the padlock she could see her fingers trembling, she was terrified but was it because of what she would see or was something about to happen? Then suddenly someone was touching her shoulder. Calling her name.

Annie's eyes flew open only to find herself staring directly into the face of the flight attendant.

"I'm sorry to wake you but we will be landing in ten minutes." She smiled at Annie as she moved on to check on the other passengers.

Annie felt ridiculous. Goodness knows what the attendant must have thought at her startled expression. She ran her hands through her hair and took some deep breaths in an effort to slow down her heart rate.

The sun was just starting to rise and as Annie looked out of the small window, she crossed her fingers.

"Here we come Kevin," she whispered under her breath.

"Keep us safe while we find you."

Chapter 43

Gavin stood patiently watching the passengers from the Manchester flight as they passed through customs. Annie had emailed a recent photo of herself, so he was confident that he would be able to pick her out from the crowd.

A dark head appeared from around the corner and as she looked up, Gavin recognised her instantly and waved. Seeing Gavin's waving figure, as she turned the corner, Annie waved back and slowly made her way through the crowd to where Gavin was standing.

"Annie! I'm so glad you're here. Was your flight okay?"

"Fine thanks. I slept through most of it."

Gavin took her holdall. "Let me carry your bag for you. You look beat. Overnight flights always do that to me."

Annie smiled, Gavin appeared to be a bit of a chatterbox.

"We'll go to the hotel first so that you can freshen up, and then head over to Comino. Are you okay with that?"

Before Annie could respond, Gavin had started speaking again. "We are going to head over to Gozo first as that is where the last official sighting of Kevin was. It's only a short trip across the water to Gozo and like I say you can freshen up at the hotel there before we head across to Comino. Our police escort is a young officer called Paul, he's waiting for us over at Gozo. He is up-to-date with your notes and he thinks he has a good idea as to the location of the hut!"

Annie was struggling to keep up with Gavin. She could feel herself panicking at the thought of losing sight of him in the crowd. As they walked past the exit, she could see a line of taxis outside, she called out to him.

"Gavin, where are we going? The exit's back there!"

He stopped and turned. "Sorry Annie, I know I'm rushing you. It's just that the helicopter is waiting."

"Helicopter?"

Gavin smiled at her wide-eyed expression, "Annie, how did you think that we were going to get to the island?"

"Well.......by boat. You said it was a short trip across the water."

"We could do but that will take longer. We only have a short window of time to get across and find Kevin. A helicopter is much quicker for what we need to do." He paused, "Crikey Annie. You look like a startled rabbit!"

Putting down her bag, he closed the gap between them in three easy strides. "Annie, you're not frightened about going up in a helicopter are you?"

She shook her head, "I don't think so, but then again, I've never been in one to know whether I'm scared or not."

Gavin laughed out loud, "Follow me. You'll be fine."

Annie kept close to Gavin. She had a feeling that she was being watched but then again, the two of them had probably looked an odd pair, stood in the middle of the departure lounge, with her looking like a frightened school kid.

"Get a grip Annie," she muttered under her breath.

Suddenly, they were out in the fresh air and ahead of her, she could see a rather large looking helicopter. She felt slightly relieved. In her mind, she had expected to see one of those small helicopters you see on films to be waiting for them. This looked more like a small plane.

Gavin boarded first, closely followed by Annie. There were already several passengers on board, some of whom she recognised from the Manchester flight. Gavin busied himself with trying to stow her holdall under the seat in front. This gave Annie the opportunity to take in her surroundings. She was starting to feel more at ease now. All of a sudden, there was a loud piercing noise. Annie and Gavin simultaneously covered their ears. Annie looked ahead to see what the source of the sound was. She was amazed to see a stewardess standing at the front of the helicopter, with a microphone in her hand, which was obviously the cause of the noise as it was creating feedback.

"Why does she have a microphone? She just needs to raise her voice and we'd hear her," whispered Annie to Gavin.

"I know. You only need to take half a dozen steps and you've reached the back of this damn thing," whispered back Gavin. "Mind you, if you think that's unnecessary, wait until the next bit!"

Annie threw him a questioning look but Gavin just pointed to the stewardess and mouthed the word, "Watch."

Feeling even more puzzled, she looked back towards the stewardess who now had a set of cue cards in her hand, which she began to read from. Safety instructions were now coming out of the microphone at ear-splitting volume. Annie looked around at the other passengers. None of them could watch the young girl as they were all trying desperately hard not to laugh!

Annie placed a hand in front of her mouth, in a feeble attempt to stifle a giggle. Gavin's shoulders were literally bouncing up and down as he tried not to laugh.

"This is the fourth time that I've seen this and I still cannot get over how bizarre it is."

Just at that point, the helicopter's rotors started to turn. Annie held on tight, expecting any moment to lift into the air leaving her stomach behind. She was taken off-guard by the fact that it started to trundle down the runway first taking a left turn, shortly followed by a right.

"Is this thing ever going to fly or is it an alternative version to getting a taxi!" muttered Annie.

Gavin laughed out loud, "I thought the exact same thing the first time."

After a few minutes, they were airborne and although

Annie wasn't sure about the sensation of being jiggled

around in a big tin bucket, she was relieved to be heading

to the island.

Gavin tapped her arm and pointed out of the window.

"See that small piece of land? That's Comino."

Annie leaned forward to get a closer look. All of the noise

from the helicopter seemed to melt away. She could

almost sense Kevin and Molly. It could have been a trick

of the light, but she felt sure that she had seen a white

light in one particular area of the island. She leant back

into her seat, and closed her eyes.

"Annie are you okay?"

She opened her eyes and nodded. The enormity of what

she was about to do had hit her head on. She hoped that

she could give Karen the closure that she needed.

Chapter 44

Gavin had organised for them to stay in a hotel on the

island of Gozo. He had deliberately picked the small town

of Mgarr, as this was the main port for the island. On

arriving at the small airport in Gozo, swift introductions

had been made to Paul who would be their police escort

for the duration of their search. A quick ten-minute drive

had brought them to their hotel and during the drive Paul

had updated them on his plans to take a boat across to the

island within the hour so that they could begin their

search.

As Annie looked out of her bedroom window at the view

across the water, se could see the small island of Comino

where they would be heading shortly. When flying over it

earlier she had been struck by the beautiful clear water

surrounding part of the island. This, Gavin had informed

her, was the Blue Lagoon.

On reading her notes, Paul had suggested that it would be

a good idea to approach the island in the same way that

Kevin had, by boat. Annie agreed that this was a sound idea. She could follow in Kevin's path and hopefully locate him. Her only concern was that in her visions, she had seen snippets of scenery but not the full picture. Her hope was, that when she arrived on the island, all would become clear.

A gentle tap at the door brought Annie back from her thoughts.

"Annie, are you ready?"

It was Gavin. He certainly was not wasting any time. They had only arrived at the hotel twenty minutes ago. Walking over to the door, Annie caught sight of her reflection in the large, decorative mirror on the wall. She had dark circles under her eyes and her face was its now usual pale complexion.

"Two minutes!" she called back.

"Okay. I'll meet you in reception. The boat is ready to take us across."

She headed into the bathroom to splash some cold water onto her face. The sting of the coldness made her whole face tingle. Patting her face dry with a large, fluffy towel, her thoughts drifted to Lisa. She had not rung home yet, partly because she did not feel that she was in good enough control of her emotions not to get upset when she spoke to them. Her heart ached. She loved Lisa as if she was the sister that she never had. Not a day had gone by when they did not talk to one another. It seemed incomprehensible that this would change so soon. Annie decided to ring her when she got back from the island in a couple of hours. Today was more a case of familiarising herself with the island. Tomorrow would be the official search.

Grabbing a thick aran sweater from her bag, Annie headed down to the foyer. Paul and Gavin were standing by the reception desk patiently waiting for her. They were both dressed in thick woollen jumpers, just like her, and both had expectant looks on their faces. Walking over to them, she felt an air of calmness come over her. *"You'll find me,"* she could hear in her head. *"Just listen for the signs."*

Well, I better had find you, thought Annie. There are a lot of people depending on me.

Smiling at Paul and Gavin, she reached out and shook Paul's hand. "Thanks again for helping us today Paul."

"I'm more than happy to help. I have to be honest though. I'm not really a believer in all this psychic stuff but I do find it interesting," he paused, "I hope I haven't offended you Annie."

Annie laughed, "Not at all. I appreciate your honesty."

He was still holding her hand. He gently squeezed it, "I think that we will get along fine."

Gavin, desperate to get across to the island, coughed loudly. "Now that we have that out of the way, can we please get on?"

Paul released Annie's hand. Smiling at Gavin's impatience he started to walk towards the exit. "We have a boat ready to take us across. The water is a little choppy today, do you mind that Annie?"

"I'll be fine thanks. I haven't exactly got great sea legs but I'm sure I'll be fine."

As they walked down to the harbour, Gavin draped an arm around Annie's shoulders, "I can't thank you enough Annie. Not everyone would drop what they are doing to come out here and help. I know Karen feels much more confident now that you are here."

Annie smiled up at Gavin, "Let's hope I can help. I can only go by what I have seen through my visions but I do feel that we will find him."

A small boat bobbed up and down at the harbour. It had been painted in some lovely bright colours and made a wonderful splash of colour against the dark blue of the sea. Annie took it as a good omen that the letters ANT were just visible from where she stood.

Paul stepped aboard first, followed by Gavin. They then both held out a hand for Annie who jumped across. She could feel the boat rocking beneath her feet. Swallowing hard, she sat down, gripping on tightly to the wooden bench that was slightly damp with the seawater spray coming over the edge. Both men laughed at her, "Annie if you go any paler, we'll think that you have turned into one of the ghosts!" Paul joked.

"I'll be fine, I'm just aclimatising myself."

Gavin sat down next to her. "You'll be fine. It only takes twenty minutes to get across."

Annie shut her eyes. Twenty minutes! She smiled weakly, "Well, let's get it over with."

Paul nodded to the captain of the boat. The engines roared into life accompanied by a strong smell of diesel fumes. The boat slowly headed out of the harbour and into open water. The earlier choppiness had eased and Annie could feel herself releasing her grip. Paul came and sat beside her. Pointing across to Comino, he laid out the initial plan for their investigation, "We'll come into the Blue Lagoon as you mention the colour of the water in your notes."

Annie nodded, "I agree. Are there any steps? I mention steps as well."

"Yes, there are. How do you want to work this when we get there Annie?"

"I'm not sure I follow what you mean."

Looking slightly sheepish, Paul leaned over so that only Annie could hear, "Do we follow you? Is it a bit like being a sniffer dog and you follow a trail?"

Smirking, Annie was tempted to make him feel even more awkward. "A sniffer psychic eh? I'll have to add that to my CV!"

Paul blushed. Annie patted his hand, "I'm only teasing. I think we just play it by ear. I'll see what I pick up but I would appreciate your help and guidance around the island."

Gavin pulled out Annie's notes. Paul held up a copy that he had as well.

"Do you need a copy Annie?" questioned Gavin.

She shook her head, "No, I'm fine thanks. I'd rather go with what I get up here," and with that she tapped the side of her head.

The engines of the boat cut out as they came into the blue lagoon. As they slowly drifted towards the sandy bay, Annie felt a strong feeling of fear come over her. She discarded it, putting it down to the imminent discovery of Kevin. Looking back out across the water to Gozo she caught sight of a small boat heading towards Comino. She pointed it out to Paul who did not seem overly concerned. "We have lots of people who come out here to sightsee. If they come onto the island, I'll ensure that they do not interfere with what we are doing."

She looked out back across the water, at the small boat. The feeling of fear waved over her again. Annie had a bad feeling about the boat and its occupants, but she also knew that there was no point in saying anything more. Paul and Gavin would probably think that she was just being silly.

Chapter 45

As Annie stepped off the boat onto the sandy bay, she had every right to feel fearful.

Through binoculars, her every movement was being followed. Sunlight glanced off the ring of the watcher. Putting down the binoculars, the ring fingered man growled across at his accomplice.

"Are you sure about your information?"

"Yes," he nodded. "The receptionist at the hotel told me yesterday about the visitor coming to look for a missing man. It's supposed to be kept quiet but you know how rumour spreads here. She couldn't help herself."

The ring fingered man picked the binoculars up and looked again at the small group making their way up the hill from the boat. As they disappeared out of view, he turned back. "If she is what they say she is, then we could have a problem. If she can find him then she may know about us."

"What can we do?"

"I have an idea."

"Look, we can't kill her as well. We've already made a mistake with the man. Please tell me you have another plan." The sound of panic in his voice was palpable.

"We will do what needs to be done to shut her up! Do you want to go to jail?"

"You said that no-one would come looking for him!"

"Well they have!" With that he shot his accomplice a hateful stare. "You are in this just as deeply as me. Do not forget that!"

They both remained quiet as they continued their trip to the island. Heading the boat towards a small cove further away from where Annie had alighted.

They would wait and watch.

Chapter 46

Walking along the dusty path, Annie was aware of Paul

and Gavin staying a few steps behind. She really was

beginning to feel like the sniffer psychic that they had

joked about earlier. As they came to the top of the incline,

she could see ahead of her a path leading down to what

looked like a group of small buildings. She could not

remember seeing them in her visions but she felt the pull

in her stomach, which was confirmation to her that she

was heading in the right direction.

Looking back at Paul and Gavin, she pointed down

towards the group of buildings.

"I want to head down, past those," she called out to them.

The men nodded and continued to follow behind Annie at

a steady pace.

"Do you think she'll find him?" whispered Paul to Gavin.

"Yes I do. We will just need to give her time. If you had

asked me a few weeks ago, if I would follow a psychic

across a small island in the hope of finding a dead

colleague, I would have told you to get your head
checked!"

Paul nodded, "I know exactly what you mean. Many of
the officers at work think I'm foolish for helping."

They both looked ahead at Annie's retreating figure as
she made her way down the hill.

"I don't know what it is about her, but I trust her
implicitly."

Paul nodded, "I agree. She doesn't appear to be someone
who would do this at the expense of other people's
emotions."

Annie turned and waved back at them. She then pointed
to something just ahead and to the right.

"She can't have found him already!"

"Let's see what it is."

They both picked up the pace and joined Annie.

"What is it?" Paul was first to question.

Annie again pointed ahead, "We're coming up to the
chapel. Look!"

Gavin followed her finger and could see a flash of white.

He looked down at his notes, "I'd forgotten about that. Is

that where he is?"

Annie shook her head, "No, but it is one of the pieces of

the trail."

They headed down to the small white chapel. It had seen

better days. Close up, the paint was peeling and weeds

were growing out of the rotten window frames. Annie and

Paul walked around one side of the building, while Gavin

walked around the other.

"Annie!" shouted Gavin.

Both Paul and Annie ran to where Gavin was standing. In

front of him was a garage. He pointed at the notes he was

holding, "Annie, you mention a garage with blue doors

and a red tractor." Annie looked at the garage. Just like

the chapel, the paint was peeling off the worn wood. As

the three of them walked up to the garage, Paul was the

first to break the silence.

"Doesn't look like there is a red tractor in there."

Gavin threw him an angry look, "So far, we have the chapel and the garage. That's pretty convincing in my book."

Annie smiled to herself, it was quite charming to have Gavin jump to her defence, especially after his cynical start with her only a few days ago. Paul glanced across at Annie.

"I didn't mean to offend you. I just would have been even more convinced if I had seen........."

Annie lifter her head to see why he had stopped talking mid sentence, "Paul, are you alright?"

Gavin smiled, he could see what Paul was seeing. "Turn around Annie and look behind you."

As she turned, a flash of red caught her eye from in between the greenery ahead of her. Paul had already walked past her and headed into the high bushes. Gavin and Annie made their way through, to find Paul standing by a tractor. A red tractor.

"I apologise Annie."

"No problem," she mumbled back. In some strange way,

she had been hoping that her visions had been wrong.

Finding Kevin dead was not, to her, a great outcome. So

far everything she had seen in her visions was coming to

fruition.

"Where now Annie?"

She closed her eyes, listening to the small voice inside her

head. That voice told her to go straight ahead. "This

way."

The mood had changed. All three of them felt as if they

were close. It had become colder and Anne was grateful

for the warmth of her thick jumper. The sky overhead was

beginning to fill with dark clouds. A gentle breeze was

rustling through the small bushes around them. As they

kept to the narrow dirt path Annie caught a familiar whiff

of cigar smoke. He stomach churned, she could not

believe that they could be getting so close so quickly.

Today was meant to be a case of familiarising herself

with the island but now she had that familiar signal that

came from Karen's mum. This was happening much

quicker than she had been prepared for. Turning to Paul

and Gavin, she warned them that they were close.

Slowing their pace at Annie's request, they kept to either

side of her. Almost as if they were protecting her.

Walking past what appeared to be some allotments on

either side of them, they approached a split in the path.

"Which way now Annie?" Paul looked at her for advice,

there was no doubting her now.

She nodded her head towards the right hand path.

"Are you sure?" asked Gavin.

"Yes, it's not far now."

"How do you know?" Paul was genuinely interested.

"Right now I feel very sick and every time I look in that

direction, I feel a strong pull in my stomach. That is my

signal, I know it may sound odd but that's how I am being

directed."

"Okay, if it works for you then let's go."

The path had become overgrown and Annie could feel the

sharp piercing of the thorny bushes as they tugged at her

ankles even through her jeans. The allotments had thinned

out. No buildings were visible.

"Annie are you sure this is the right way?" You could hear the disappointment in Gavin's words.

Looking ahead, Annie could see what looked like a small thicket of trees. As she stared, she again felt that familiar pull in her gut. It was such a strong feeling now that she was physically holding her stomach as if she was in pain. She was sure that she could see a shimmer of light ahead of her. Almost like a heat wave.

The light was diminishing as storm clouds gathered above now. Paul was worried about how Annie was reacting to the 'feelings' that she had. She looked in pain and to him this did not seem right, he voiced his concern. "Annie we will need to head back soon, you are starting to look ill with this plus the weather is starting to turn."

"Just five more minutes, please?" she begged.

He looked at her face, she was desperate to continue. He was torn between his concern for her and the potential for finding Kevin. He reluctantly agreed, "Okay you have fifteen more minutes and then we head back - no arguments."

She nodded back, grateful to him for letting her continue.

Annie's steps were now more urgent. She could feel sobs

catching her throat. Salty tears were running down her

face. Kevin was close. She knew it.

The thicket was in front of them now. Annie pushed her

way through, thorns catching her face and hair but she

didn't care. Then, as she broke through the tangle of

bushes, there was the outbuilding directly in front of her.

Paul walked past her, "Is this it?"

She nodded. The blue door with its shiny padlock stared

back at her. Not yet ready to release its secret to the small

group in front of it. Gavin grabbed hold of her hand, she

could feel the tremble of his body as he spoke.

"It's just like you said Annie," he whispered.

Paul tugged at the padlock. It was firmly locked. Annie

moved forward, and seeing a small gap in the wood, she

slowly put one eye up towards the thin slit, and looked

through. A leg was the first thing she saw. Blood was

pounding in her ears. She tried to see more, and then fell

to her knees, wrapping her arms around herself as she

gagged. She had caught sight of Kevin. It had not been a

pretty picture.

Paul took out a gun from inside his jacket. Both Annie

and Gavin stared at him in surprise.

"Precaution," he smiled grimly.

Gavin and Annie stepped back as Paul aimed his gun at

the padlock. The ring of the gunshot ran out across the

island.

Tentatively opening the door, the first thing that hit Paul

was the smell. Covering his mouth and nose with his

sleeve, he pushed open the door to its full extent. In the

corner lay what remained of Kevin. Rodents and time had

taken their revenge, however there was no mistaking that

the body laid against the back wall of the hut was Kevin.

The brown curly hair matched the picture that he had seen

of Kevin, for now it was all the confirmation that he

needed. If Gavin felt up to it, he could make a positive

identification.

Paul walked out from the small wooden hut and took a large gulp of fresh air. Nodding at Annie, he turned to Gavin. "It's Kevin. I'll be honest with you, he is probably not in the best state to identify him right now and I think you should wait, but I will understand if you want to go in.

Gavin got as far as the entrance. The smell was enough to make him throw up, but the sight of Kevin tipped him over the edge. Annie stayed where she was. She did not need to see. She could hear Paul on the phone requesting a helicopter as well as extra manpower.

"They will be here in ten minutes. Annie, are you alright? Do you need anything?"

"I'm fine thanks. I wouldn't mind getting away from here though. Would you mind if I walk back to the boat and wait for you there?"

"Will you find your way back on your own?"

She nodded. Gavin needed to stay with Paul. He had already rung Karen to briefly advise her that they had found Kevin. It had been a stilted conversation and Annie was glad that she had not been required to speak to Karen.

It would have been too much to handle at that moment.

"We'll catch you up as soon as we can. Are you sure you

are okay to go back on your own?" Paul was worried

about how Annie would be feeling after their grim

discovery.

Annie nodded, she needed to get away from the sight of

Kevin. She had done what she had needed to do and now

there was nothing more she could help with.

Chapter 47

It had become much colder on the island. The sky had darkened and the beautiful clear blue sky of earlier had long since gone. There was a sense of tension in the air, which was making Annie jittery. Walking quickly, in an attempt to warm herself up as well as to distance herself from what she had just seen, she suddenly found herself back at the white chapel. As she slowly walked around the chapel, letting her hands run along the rough, uneven surface of the stonework, she became aware of the feeling of being watched. Glancing behind her nervously she could not see anything, but the feeling stayed with her. She shook her head, her nerves were all over the place after finding Kevin that must be what it was.

In the distance, she could hear the dull thud of the helicopter as it headed towards the island. Continuing to walk alongside the chapel, she heard a noise from behind her. Turning quickly, she let out a startled cry at the sight of a man just behind her standing quite still.

"Apologies for startling you. I live here on the island and I was just taking a walk."

Annie felt scared. She did not know why, but every nerve in her body told her to run and run now!

"I'm sorry, I wasn't aware that anyone lived on the island. My friends, who I have just left, said that no-one was here." She made a point of mentioning her friends so that this stranger knew that she was not completely on her own.

A dark look crossed his face, "Well, they were wrong. I look after the hotel." He pointed across to where the hotel was. That was when Annie saw it. The ring! It was just like the one in her visions. She stumbled backwards, fear gripping her. What was he doing here? Did he know that they had already found Kevin?

"I'm terribly sorry but I can't stop to talk. A boat is waiting to take me back," she turned to walk away and bumped straight into another man. She had not heard him come up behind her. Panic was rising. She could feel her heart pounding, despite the cold she could feel a trickle of sweat running down her back. Annie made to walk past him but he stepped in front of her again, blocking her way. The man with the ring was now directly behind her and without warning, he put an arm around her neck. She was stuck in a vice-like grip.

"What do you want?" she managed to say.

He leaned forward, his mouth millimetres away from her ear. She could smell his foul breath, she wanted to gag. His lips now touching her ear. She was terrified, she should have stayed with Paul and Gavin, it had been foolish to come back on her own. What she needed to do now was find a way to escape from these two monsters – Kevin's killers.

"So, did you find what you were looking for?" he whispered into her ear.

Annie knew that there was no point in pretending.

"Yes we did. You won't get away with it you know. My friends will be here any minute."

"Well, in that case, we had better move hadn't we?"

He released his grip. "Don't think about running away. We'd catch you."

Annie wasn't so sure about that. She was a reasonable

athlete and if she could get a good head start then she

might just be able to get away. Something in her look

must have given away what she was thinking as without

warning he slapped her hard across the face, knocking her

to the ground with the force of the blow. She landed hard,

hitting the side of her face on the rocky path.

Annie lay stunned. Tentatively touching her face, she

pulled her fingers away quickly at the feeling of

dampness. Looking at her fingers, she could see that they

were covered in blood. She was starting to feel dizzy and

sick. It was cold, becoming darker and there was no sign

of Paul or Gavin. Where were they?

The ring man pulled her up roughly by the arm. "Move!"

He pushed her hard in the back and she felt something

sharp prodding her. He had a knife!

They were now heading away from the chapel, along a

dirt path. Annie tried to memorise landmarks as she went.

Behind her, she could hear the two men quietly arguing.

"I thought you were just going to scare her!"

"It's gone too far for that. You saw how she took them straight to the hut. She'll lead them to us next. We need to get rid of her!"

Annie had never felt so scared in her life. She could not think straight. Her head hurt and the dizziness was worse. A group of small buildings appeared next to what looked like an old fort. Annie stumbled over the rough path and then felt herself being pulled back by her hair.

"Don't do anything stupid!" he warned her.

The knife was just inches away from her throat. He pushed her roughly towards the buildings. Walking into what looked like a courtyard, she could see lights twinkling across the water on Gozo. It was getting dark quickly. Suddenly, the helicopter flew over on its way to collect Kevin. Despite herself, she sobbed.

"Scared? So you should be!" laughed ring man. He slowly stroked her face with the knife, she could feel the sharpness of the blade against her skin. He pushed her against a wall, her back pressed hard against the rough stonework, the woollen jumper she was wearing protecting her back from being grazed by its hardness. He leaned into her, pressing his body against her, his stinking

breath making her gag.

"If you are psychic, then perhaps you already know what

is about to happen." He laughed at his own joke. "You are

very pretty. Perhaps my friend and I should have some

fun first before we kill you."

Ring man's accomplice attempted to step in between him

and Annie, "What are you doing? Isn't it enough that you

have killed once? Why are you doing this?"

What happened next made Annie's blood run cold.

Callously, ring man plunged the knife into his associate's

stomach. As he dropped to his knees in front of Annie,

ring man stood over him, the knife in his hand darkened

with blood.

"I need to get rid of all the evidence. You shouldn't have

questioned me!" He crouched down to whisper something

to the dying man, his attention momentarily diverted from

Annie.

Without thinking of the consequences, Annie took the

opportunity and bolted. She had no idea where she was

headed. She just knew that she needed to run and run fast!

A determination moved through Annie and her tired

limbs. A determination to get away and to live.

She rounded the corner of the low buildings, her legs felt

weak but she knew that she needed to move on. Ahead of

her was the fort, to the right was another path that would

take her around to the front of the buildings. Looking

back, she could see nothing but could hear heavy

footsteps heading her way.

"Come on Kevin, help me!" she whispered. Her gut-

instinct told her to turn right. She broke into a sprint. Up

ahead there was a fork in the road. As if on automatic

pilot, she took a left. She did not dare turn around. Ring

man was a good runner and he was catching up fast.

Unfortunately for Annie, he knew the island very well. As

she rounded a corner, he suddenly sprinted out from some

woodland just to the left of her. He was breathing heavily

but his pace did not slow.

Annie screamed. She had to pick up speed but the blow to

her head earlier was making her feel dizzy and uncoordinated. He was catching her up. She could hear his heavy steps. He made a last effort to catch her, and lunging towards her he managed to grab hold of her jumper. She jerked backwards, falling. Then a sharp pain. She couldn't move. There was a blinding pain in her leg. What had just happened?

He stood up awkwardly, looking down at her, "Why did you have to run away?"

Annie was feeling faint. Reaching out her hand to the source of the pain on her thigh, she felt it wet and sticky. He was starting to swim in front of her. She knew that any second she would faint.

"Why?" she whispered. "Why did you kill Kevin?"

He stared down at her and laughed grimly, "A case of mistaken identity. He could have lived but he chose to run away as well. I'm not a killer you know. I just wanted to make right a wrong. He got in the way and now he is dead." For the first time, he looked scared. "I can't get caught for what I did. I have no choice."

"But your friend?" cried Annie.

"He was weak. He would have told someone eventually."

Annie felt herself slipping into unconsciousness. She tried hard to pull herself back from the darkness enveloping her. That was when a slight movement caught the corner of her eye. She strained her eyes in the darkness to see what had caused it. A faint outline could be seen in the shadows. Paul! Her heart skipped a beat. She turned to look at ring man. He had not noticed Paul as far as she could tell. She needed to distract him so that Paul could get closer. Unfortunately just at that moment he turned and caught sight of Paul's shadowy figure. Dragging Annie by the hair, he pulled her up into a standing position. She screamed with the pain.

"Shut up!" he yelled at her. "This is all your fault. Why did you have to come here?"

Paul walked forward, his gun held out in front of him. "Let her go."

Annie screamed again, as ring man pushed the tip of the knife very slowly into her leg. Paul stopped. He was unable to get a clear shot. Annie's eyes were misting over, she felt weak and suddenly very, very tired. As she took one last look at Paul, she thought she saw him make

a slight nod with his head.

As she slipped into unconsciousness, she felt

sure that she heard a loud bang then a sudden weight

forcing all the breath out of her.

Chapter 48

"Annie! Annie! Can you hear me? Please open your
eyes."

A roaring noise filled Annie's ears and as she slowly
opened her eyes, there appeared to be lights flying above
her head.

"It's a rescue helicopter Annie. We're taking you to
hospital."

Gavin was kneeling beside her. They were on the dirt
path. She turned her head and could see Paul with another
policeman who was in uniform. They were standing over
ring man.

"Is he dead?" she whispered.

"No," Gavin shook his head, "badly wounded but he will
live to see the rest of his life behind bars."

"I feel very sleepy," whispered Annie.

"Just hang in there Annie, we'll get you to hospital soon."

Annie fell back into unconsciousness.

Chapter 49

Pain was the first thing that Annie was aware of on waking up. It felt as if her whole body ached in some form, her face felt tight and tender when she touched it but the worst pain of all was in her leg. She wasn't brave enough to touch it to find out what the damage was but even if she moved her leg just slightly, the pain was excruciating. She closed her eyes, trying to breathe through the pain. After a few minutes, she opened her eyes again to take in her surroundings. Well, I'm alive, was her first thought. As she slowly looked around the room she was in, she observed that there were a number of machines that appeared to be linked to her in some way that were all giving reassuring beeps. She couldn't remember how she had got here, she felt groggy but wasn't sure if it was through drugs that had been administered to her or just the effects of what had happened on the island. She suddenly saw a vision of Kevin lying in the hut. A sob escaped from her as she started to remember the events of a few hours ago.

Gavin was asleep, slumped in a chair beside her bed, gently snoring but at the sound of Annie crying, he instantly woke up.

"Hey, how are you doing?" he ran a hand through his hair.

"What happened Gavin?"

He leaned over and took hold of Annie's hand. "We got to the boat and you weren't there. Paul rang the officers at the hut to check if you had gone back to find us. That's when they said that they had seen three people walking along a path not far from the hut, when they were flying over. They couldn't be sure that it was you but Paul knew that no one else had been on the island when we had arrived, so he instantly sent everyone on a search. We walked back to the chapel and saw signs of a scuffle, plus we found this," he held up Annie's bracelet.

"I hadn't realised that it had fallen off."

"Paul called ahead to the other officers and after a few wrong turns, we managed to track you down. You were obviously injured when we arrived as you were lying on the ground but when we were spotted, the man pulled you up and held you at knifepoint. One of the officers shot the man who was holding you. He'll live but if I have my way he'll never get outside prison."

"Why did he do it? I vaguely remember him saying that he had mistaken Kevin for someone else but it's still quite fizzy up here," she tapped the side of her head.
Gavin sat back in his chair. "It's a bit of an odd situation but it was all to do with mistaking Kevin for a paedophile," he looked at Annie. "Yes Annie you were right with that link. I honestly don't know how you do it." He shifted in his chair in an attempt to get more comfortable. "Long story short, his niece was very badly abused by this paedophile who had been going around the islands for months unidentified. The police had a lucky break a few weeks earlier where one of the children had been able to provide them with a good enough description that they were able to put a decent photofit together. Our friend was determined to get revenge. Initially all he wanted to do was scare him. Unfortunately for Kevin, his looks weren't dissimilar hence the mistaken identity. It then got out of hand and sadly as you know Kevin died.

Apparently this man is well-known for his violent tendencies and has reportedly been responsible for some other brutal attacks on people over the years however none until now have led to someone's death."

He leaned forward, sadness etched in his face. "Annie, I am so sorry for what has happened. You know that I would not knowingly have put you in danger."

"I know you wouldn't. At least I'm alive and in one piece." She tried to straighten herself up in bed and winced at the pain. "So, what's the story with my leg it hurts like hell?"

"You have been very lucky although I appreciate you probably don't think so at the moment! I won't lie to you, it is a very nasty stab wound but given time and physio you will be fine." He fastened the bracelet around her wrist as he spoke.

"The downside is that you will have to stay here for a couple of days before you can fly though."

"I can't! I need to get home."

"It's okay, everyone knows back home what has happened. Your friend Lisa told me to tell you that she isn't going anywhere."

Annie smiled, "Can I call her?"

"Yes of course. There's a phone just by your bed. I have to say, she's got a bit of a temper on her hasn't she? Both she and Richard really let rip!"

Annie laughed, "Well, you did promise to keep me safe. I don't think a stab wound and a bump to the head fit into that category!" she grimaced as she moved.

"Annie?"

"What is it Gavin?" There was something about his tone that sounded sad.

"I haven't told Karen about the state of Kevin's body. I didn't want to upset her. The post-mortem will be carried out tomorrow and then I can take him back."

"So what have you told her?"

"Just that we found him exactly as you had said in your notes and that he looked very peaceful," he paused. Annie looked into his face. Poor man, she thought, this has been just as hard for him.

"Take your time Gavin, this has been a difficult few days."

He played with the bracelet now back safely around her wrist. "It's very pretty. The leaves all intertwine."

"Yes, it's a tree of life bracelet. At least that's what I call it. Lisa gave it to me as a birthday present a few years ago."

"Very apt, considering it saved your life."

"What else did you say to Karen?"

"I told her that it looked as if he had died from a very bad injury that had led to blood poisoning."

"How did she take it?"

"Very calmly. She already knew in her heart that he was dead. All she wanted was for us to find him and bring him home."

"So what's the problem Gavin?"

"I don't want her seeing Kevin as he is. It's not the last image she should have of him."

"Has she asked to see him?"

Gavin shook his head.

"Well, let's see what happens. She is a very strong woman and if you have to Gavin, you will have to tell her the truth. She's not stupid."

"I know, it's just...."

"What? What is it Gavin?"

He leaned back in his chair, dark circles making his eyes appear incredibly sunken. She had not noticed that before. He looked worn out. Wiping a hand across his face, he looked directly at Annie.

"It's my fault Annie!"

"What?"

"I was so desperate that Kevin got the deal that I pushed him to stay here another couple of days. If he'd gone home as planned, then he may still be alive."

"You don't know that."

"It didn't help though, did it? He may well have got away from here before that madman saw him." He slouched back in his chair, a beaten man.

A small tap at the door broke the silence.

"Come in!" called Annie.

Paul poked his head around the door. "Are you up for a visitor?"

"Come in Paul, it's good to see you."

He came round the other side of the bed. "How do you feel?"

"Sore, but I'll live. Thank you for what you did."

He shook his head, "No Annie. It's you that we should be thanking. You've certainly opened my eyes in regards to psychics. You're also quite a tough nut aren't you!"

"I've been called worse," she joked.

The three of them spent the next half hour finalising details of what had happened on the island that night, as well as confirming travel arrangements for Annie.

"You won't need to come back to make a statement. We have everything we need, although I hope it hasn't put you off visiting Gozo in the future. It really is a beautiful place."

Annie shook her head, "I'd love to come back. Maybe in the summer, when it's a bit warmer," she joked.

"We would be honoured," Paul took her hand and kissed it. "Thank you Annie. You are a very brave lady."

Annie flushed, she hardly thought that screaming like a banshee was brave!

"We'll escort you to the airport the day after tomorrow."

"Thank you Paul, for everything."

As he left the room, Annie looked across at Gavin, "Go back to the hotel and get some sleep."

"Are you sure?"

"I'm not going anywhere. I've got some calls to make and then no doubt there will be some poking and prodding from that doctor who keeps peaking through the glass!"

Gavin laughed, "Yes, he was the one who looked after you when you arrived. I told him to wait a while before he started on you again."

After Gavin left, Annie called home. The relief at hearing Lisa's voice made Annie breakdown. Between sobs, she briefly outlined the events of finding Kevin but left out a large part of the story relating to her being injured. Neither of them wanted to end the call but Annie was exhausted.

"Richard will go mad when he finds out he has missed your call."

"Tell him I love him and will see him soon."

"You used the L word!" screeched Lisa, "You must have had a very nasty bang to the head."

"Watch it lady," giggled Annie.

As she lay back in her hospital bed, she felt sure that there was a faint smell of cigar smoke. Smiling to herself, she closed her eyes and for the first time, in a long time, had a dreamless sleep.

Chapter 50

Paul and Gavin had kept their promise and exactly two days later, Annie was on the plane headed back home. Much to Annie's embarrassment, she was transported to the plane by ambulance and Paul had organised a small police escort for her. Gavin had travelled with her to the airport and it had been an emotional farewell for them both as she arrived at the airport.

"Don't blame yourself for what happened," she whispered into his ear as he hugged her.

"It's hard not to," he replied.

Her heart went out to him, only time would heal the guilt that he felt. Time and perhaps forgiveness from Karen although Annie knew from conversations that she had previously had with Karen that she did not blame Gavin for what had happened. In Karen's own words *'Kevin is a grown man, he could have said no'.*

As the plane began its final approach into Inverness, Annie leaned over to take a look at the lights twinkling over the city. Pressing her forehead to the window she felt relief at finally being home. She leaned back in her seat as the plane landed back on Scottish soil, the bump of the landing sending a shot of pain through her leg. She shut her eyes at the pain.

"Are you ready Annie?" It was the stewardess who had looked after Annie since her arrival on the plane. Much to Annie's embarrassment, she required a wheelchair as she could not walk on her leg. She had been advised to take it slowly and steadily as there had been a large amount of muscle damage where the knife had entered her thigh. Being dependent on other people was not something that sat well with Annie. Gavin had organised the first class return flight and Annie felt sure that he must have slipped them something extra as she had been treated like royalty for the whole journey back.

As she was wheeled through into arrivals, she caught sight of Richard. A sob caught the back of her throat. She was home and he was such a welcome sight, just seeing him made her realise how much she cared for him. Annie was finding it all far too emotional and it did not help that people were staring at her. She must have looked a sight she thought, in a wheelchair, a black eye and a nasty graze on her cheek. Hardly a glamorous entrance. The stewardess leaned forward and whispered in Annie's ear, "I'm guessing that rather good looking man is waiting for you?"

Annie nodded, a huge smile spreading across her face, "Yes he is."

"Well, let's not keep him waiting then!"

Richard strode across, he couldn't wait any longer. He bent down and took hold of Annie's face, taking in the bruises and grazes across her cheeks and eye. He gently kissed her on the lips, almost as if he was scared that he would hurt her already tender face. Annie was not used to such public demonstrations of affection and by now was feeling total embarrassment.

"I think I can leave you in safe hands now," joked the stewardess.

"Thank you for looking after me."

"No problem Annie, it was an absolute pleasure."

Richard stood up and walked behind the wheelchair, he slowly pushed Annie through the airport to the exit, taking care not to hurt her damaged leg. As they arrived at the exit, Annie noticed that his car was parked just outside the door. She turned her head and raised an eyebrow at him.

"Are you flouting the airport parking rules!" she joked.

"Gavin arranged for special privileges. It appears that your wish is his command."

Annie laughed, "I'll have to remember that."

Richard walked round to the front of the chair and bent down, looking up at Annie he gently stroked her face, "Are you ready to go home now?"

Annie nodded, her eyes brimming with tears, "Yes please," she whispered.

Richard effortlessly lifted Annie from her chair and carried her out to the car.

Driving back to Dornoch, they sat in silence, holding hands whenever possible. Annie leaned back and closed her eyes. All the tension and upset from the past few days melting away. *I'm home*, she smiled to herself.

Chapter 51

Dan opened the door wide to let in Richard and Annie.

"Welcome home m'lady. I see that you are now demanding to be carried everywhere!" Dan joked but his face showed the concern that he was feeling.

"Lisa is going to have a fit when she sees the state of you! You didn't tell us about the facial improvements."

"Shut up Dan!" laughed Annie, "Is she awake?"

Dan nodded. "I was under strict instructions to wake her once Richard rang from the airport to say that you were on your way. Planned out to the final detail it was. Pick up and collect, telephone calls and then wake up her highness."

Richard carried Annie through to the living room. Annie's eyes misted over at the sight before her. Welcome home banners and balloons adorned the walls. Bonnie, with a very swollen belly was laid out in front of the fire. The best sight of all was Lisa, propped up with a sparkle in her eyes and huge smile on her face. At face value, she looked great and anyone who didn't know her would

never suspect that she was dying from cancer. Richard
had warned her in the car that the meds had been pushed
up an extra notch on Gordon's instructions, in an effort to
make things easier as the pain had become much worse.

Lisa's brilliant smile vanished when she saw the full
extent of Annie's injuries. "You didn't tell me about all
this," she scolded.
Richard placed Annie gently on the sofa beside Lisa. She
leaned over and held Annie's face in her hands, gently
stroking the bruising.
"Does it hurt?"
"Not much." She nearly said *it could have been much
worse* but stopped herself. She had not told any of them
the full story while she was recuperating in hospital.
Annie knew that they all would have fretted until she got
home.

Lisa narrowed her eyes, " Keeping anything from us
young lady?"
The way she said it made Annie realise that they had
found out more since they had last spoken.

"Before you dig yourself a large hole Annie, you should be warned that we all had a very long chat with Gavin earlier. He rang to say that he had seen you safely aboard," warned Dan, while at the same time making a hangman gesture behind Lisa's back.

"I know what you are doing Dan!" laughed Lisa. "Pour Annie a whisky, then she can tell us all the gory details."

Bonnie gently thumped her tail and lifted her head as if to welcome Annie.

"Hey there old lady, how have you been?"

"She's got a couple of weeks left until the puppies are born," Richard stroked Bonnie's swollen tummy, "She's missed you."

"We all have," smiled Lisa.

Dan walked through carrying a tray laden with glasses and nibbles.

"Hungry?"

"Starving."

"Good, we've got a big pot of stovies on the go. They'll be ready in about twenty minutes." He handed out a glass of whisky to everyone. Raising his own in a toast, he grinned at Annie, "Welcome back missus, we've missed you."

"Hear, hear!" chorused Richard and Lisa.

The room was silent for a moment as they each sipped from their glass and then they all seemed to start talking at once. They wanted to know exactly what had happened over in Comino.

"Spare no details, we want to hear everything." encouraged Dan.

Annie raised an eyebrow, there were some things that she thought were better left unsaid. She just hoped that Gavin had thought the same.

As she told her story, Lisa held on tight to her hand, while Richard kept a protective arm around her shoulders. Occasionally Lisa would stop her and make her go over certain parts again, which Annie knew was her way of drawing more out of her. Dan kept plying Annie with food and drink. The warmth of the fire along with too much whisky, was making her feel sleepy.

"I think it's time we took you to bed," Richard stood up, ready to lift up Annie and carry her upstairs.

"I can walk!" she protested, but winced as soon as she started to put weight on her leg.

"Ten out of ten for effort but for tonight, the only way that you are getting up those stairs is if I carry you!"

Annie let herself be swept up in Richard's arms. Leaning her head on his shoulder, she whispered, "I could get used to this."

He chuckled, "Good."

Tucked up in bed, Annie heard a gentle tap on the door. Lisa popped her head around the door, "Can I come in?"

Annie patted the empty space next to her on the bed. Richard had gone downstairs to make them both a hot drink.

Lisa lay down beside Annie, "So what did you leave out?" she quizzed.

"You always were far too intuitive Lisa."

Lisa hugged her friend, "Gavin alluded to you being threatened. He explained that's why you ran. Did they do anything to you Annie, before you ran away?"

Annie shook her head, "No. They threatened to, but I ran. I think I got away lightly really."

"What happens now to Kevin?"

"Well, they were holding the post mortem on the mainland and then they were going to release his body back to Karen. You know something Lisa? She really is a brave woman."

Lisa smiled, "She's not the only one who's brave. Look at what you have just experienced!"

"I'm so glad to be home Lisa. I'm really sorry that I was longer than I said." Annie was starting to cry.

Lisa gently wiped away Annie's tears, "You're here now and in one piece. That's all that matters. We were all so worried about you Annie, especially when we heard that you had been stabbed. It took all of our efforts to stop Richard getting on the next flight out there."

"I just kept thinking that it would be so unfair if I were to end up stuck out there for weeks!"

Lisa laughed, "I think Gavin has pulled many strings to get you out of there. Mind you, he was more worried that you would just get up and hobble out of your own accord."

As they both laughed, Richard walked in, "Well, two ladies in my bed! What will the neighbours say?"

"Good luck!" joked Dan as he came up behind Richard. "Come on love, it's time you were in bed. You and Annie can catch up tomorrow."

Lisa leaned over and gently kissed her friend on the forehead, "Welcome back you," she whispered.

As Richard got into bed beside her, Annie started to cry. The relief at coming home and seeing Lisa obviously getting worse was all too much for her. Richard enveloped her in his arms, gently stroking her hair. He kept quiet, knowing that she needed this moment to release all the tension that had built up over the past few days. As the sobs subsided, he gently placed a finger under her chin and lifted it up. She stared into his eyes, happy to be here lying in his arms.

"I love you,' she whispered.

"Thank goodness for that," he chuckled. "I wish I could have been there. Perhaps you wouldn't have got hurt."

Annie shook her head, "It doesn't matter what happened. I'm here now. That's all that matters."

"I love you Annie. Don't ever leave me again." He pulled her closer, as if making sure that she wouldn't run away.

As Annie lay there, listening to Richard's steady breathing as he slept. She could not help but think of Karen. How must she be feeling? To know that your husband has been murdered and to be having his baby. That was a huge ask of anyone. Turning her head to look at Richard, she knew that he was the one she wanted to be with. She was a very, very lucky person and she would make sure that she never forgot that.

Chapter 52

The next few days followed a pattern of Annie receiving

daily visits from the physiotherapist that Gavin had

arranged. Progress was slow but she had the comfort of

knowing that longer term she would get back the full use

of her leg.

Sadly Lisa's condition was deteriorating at a rapid rate.

Gordon and Rhona were insistent that they be the main

medical carers for Lisa which was a great comfort to them

all but it also made them realise that time was running out

as well.

Dan stayed close to Lisa's side almost as if he was

attached by some invisible piece of string. It hurt Annie

knowing that there was absolutely nothing that she could

do to stop the inevitable. She would watch them as he lay

beside her on top of the bed that they had brought into the

lounge. Lisa wanted to be 'amongst all the noise and

chatter' as she put it, so it made sense to have her bed

where she could see everyone and more importantly, they could keep a close eye on her.

Gordon and Rhona had just arrived as Annie was seeing out the physiotherapist. They made their way through to where Lisa was and Annie followed slowly behind on her crutches. As she joined them in the lounge, Gordon was joking about the fact that the two of them had to do everything together.

"I've never seen so many medical people in one home. Only you two could end up with the house turned into a medical centre!"

"She always did try to outdo me," laughed Lisa, "I think getting stabbed was a tad excessive though."

Gordon roared with laughter. He never ceased to be amazed at how upbeat Lisa remained considering how ill she now was. A large part of it, he knew, was down to the strong bond that Annie, Lisa, Dan and now Richard had. If only all of his patients could have such a relationship that kept them supported at times like these.

Rhona walked through, carrying two hot mugs of tea, "Here you are ladies," she passed them each a mug.

"By the way, have you seen the snowdrops outside? They're just beginning to pop their heads open."

A look passed between Lisa and Annie. Rhona could not know the significance of her statement but the girls smiled at one another. Lisa had managed to stay alive longer than any of them had thought possible.

Dan walked through from the kitchen with a huge grin on his face, "I think it's time we gave Alistair a call. It looks like Bonnie has gone into labour!"

Everyone seemed to burst into action at the same time. Gordon and Rhona ran through to look after Bonnie. Dan was on the phone to Alistair. Only Lisa and Annie remained still.

"What are you thinking Lisa?" asked Annie although she already had a good idea.

Lisa smiled gently back at her dearest friend, "New life in the house Annie. It seems rather fitting don't you think?"

Annie knew exactly what she meant. They had both always felt that for every death, a new life was introduced into the world.

"It's not time yet," whispered Annie gripping tightly onto her friend's hand.

"No, not yet but we both know that time is running out. We'll take one day at a time now - yes?"

Annie nodded, "One day at a time."

"Go and call Dan, I want to see what's happening through there!"

Bonnie had taken up residence in Lisa's dining room a few days earlier. The boys had moved the dining table off to one side to give more room. There was a chair close to where Bonnie was lying so Dan carried Lisa over to the chair and settled her. She was too weak to walk, a few steps exhausted her, and it was distressing to see. Annie hobbled behind the pair of them and sat on the edge of the chair next to Lisa.

A knock at the door signalled the arrival of Alistair. He walked through to the dining room and grinning at Gordon, he joked, "Come on, let a professional in. You human doctors know nothing when it comes to bedside manners for animals."

"Her contractions are close together now," advised
Rhona.

"Why thank you nurse. Do you have the hot water and
towels at the ready?"

Annie and Lisa burst out laughing. Gordon and Alistair
had been close friends since high school and they both
had a devillish sense of humour. The knew that Rhona
had her work cut out for her whenever they got started.

Annie had already rung Richard to warn him about
Bonnie. The office was only a few minutes away from
Lisa and Dan's home so it was no surprise when he came
bounding through the back door, bringing in a blast of
cold air with him from outside. Quickly shutting the door
to keep the warmth in, he came up behind Annie.

"Anything happen yet?"

She shook her head, "Not yet but Alistair thinks it will be
soon."

"Oh Annie, look!" cried out Lisa.

Annie turned, just in time to see a miniature Bonnie being
born. "Oh clever girl Bonnie!"

Alistair turned and smiled, "It's a girl!"

A few minutes later, another two puppies were born.

"Two more girls!" called out Alistair.

"Great! Overrun by females," joked Dan.

"Bonnie is fine," assured Alistair to Annie, "The puppies seem strong and are feeding, so I suggest we just let mum get on with it."

All of them were reluctant to leave Bonnie and the puppies alone but they could see that she was managing fine. Taking a last look at them before they left, Gordon and Rhona turned to Annie, "If you need a home for one of them then we would love to have one."

"Aren't you both busy working though? It would be quite difficult to look after a puppy if you are out all day" asked Annie.

Gordon and Rhona smiled at each other, "Well, Rhona won't be working for much longer,"

Annie looked puzzled, "How come? I thought you loved working at the hospital?"

Rhona grinned back, "I do but I've decided to take some leave. I'm pregnant!"

Annie let out a whoop of delight, "Oh Rhona that's wonderful. I'm so pleased for you both. Why didn't you tell us?"

"Well, with all that was going on, I thought it best to keep it quiet for now. I'm only twelve weeks pregnant and after what happened last time, I didn't want to tempt fate."

Annie understood completely. Rhona had miscarried last year when she was only ten weeks pregnant. She could appreciate her reluctance to announce too early the fact that she was pregnant again.

"Have you told Lisa yet?" she asked.

Rhona shook her head, "No, I didn't think it was appropriate."

"Go and tell her now, she will absolutely delighted. It will mean a lot to her."

She gave Rhona a huge hug which was no easy thing to do considering she was leaning on one crutch. Gordon laughed at her, "Watch you don't fall over!" he joked.

Once everyone had left, Annie walked through to the dining room and after a bit of difficulty, she managed to manoeuvre herself onto the floor. Gently stroking

Bonnie's head, she watched the puppies' little bodies

wriggle as they nuzzled Bonnie.

"Well done Bonnie. You're a mum now."

Bonnie gazed up at Annie, an owner to dog exchange, by

gaze only, that they did so well. A gentle thump of her

tail letting Annie know that she was content.

Chapter 53

It did not take long for Bonnie to move herself and the pups into the lounge. It was now becoming a very busy room and it was good for everyone to have the distraction of the puppies. Dan and Richard made a huge fuss of them and there was one little pup that had become very attached to Lisa. Bonnie would let Lisa hold the puppy on the bed beside her, just occasionally checking up on Lisa by plopping her head onto her bed and giving her pup a lick. It was an extremely touching thing to watch and it reminded Annie yet again of what a strong bond that they all had with each other including Bonnie.

It was a beautiful sunny day outside although still bitterly cold. Gordon and Rhona had just left and the house was quiet for a change. The rays of sun were picking out the colours from the stained-glass window in the lounge and casting a rainbow of colours across Lisa. Annie observed the contented picture of Lisa as she gently held the puppy. Her stomach lurched, she had a feeling that today would be the day that Lisa passed but she hoped that she was wrong. She had not voiced her thoughts to either Richard or Dan, she would rather that they carry on as normal. She could hear them talking in the kitchen as they made some lunch, a rare moment for Lisa and Annie where they were completely on their own as Dan hardly ever left Lisa's side now.

"You look tired Lisa, do you need anything?"

Lisa shook her head, "No I'll just rest my eyes," she looked across at Annie, "I'm very cold Annie, can you get me another blanket please?"

Annie's leg was slowly getting stronger and she was trying to use it as often as she could.

"No problem, just give me a minute to get up," she groaned as she got to her feet.

"Drama queen!" muttered Lisa.

"Love you too," laughed Annie.

The blanket box was at the other end of the room and it took Annie a few minutes to walk over, open the box and pull out a thick blanket.

"This should be just fine for madam,' she joked as she hobbled back to the bed.

She hesitated, there was something about the way Lisa looked in her sleep that made Annie know that she was gone.

"Lisa?" A rush of warm air blew into her face, "I love you Lisa," she whispered.

Slowly placing the blanket around her friend, she tucked her in and placed a kiss on her forehead. "Be happy Lisa," she whispered through her tears.

Annie slowly walked into the kitchen where Dan and Richard were putting the finishing touches to lunch. Dan was first to look up. On seeing the expression on Annie's face, he shook his head. "No - not yet!"

Annie nodded.

Dan slowly walked through to the living room with Annie and Richard following at a respectful distance. They stood in the doorway as he gently cradled Lisa in his arms, rocking backwards and forwards, tears silently rolling down his face, he looked up at them both and smiled. "At least she got to see the snowdrops."

"Yes she did," smiled Annie.

The three of them held each other's hands and looked down at the serene face of their beloved Lisa while the sun continued to cast a colourful rainbow over her.

Chapter 54

Lisa's funeral was as she had requested it to be, a colourful affair. *A day of celebration is what I want. I don't want you to mourn, I don't want you to cry,* she had stated.

All of their friends wore rainbow coloured scarves and ties and even Bonnie had a rainbow collar. The funeral was held in Dornoch Cathedral and was a simple and moving ceremony. Yet again Annie was reminded of how many lives Lisa had touched during her thirty short years. She sat between Dan and Richard with Bonnie at her feet and listened to the kind words that everyone had to say. The local school choir sang an incredibly moving version of Lisa's favourite hymn 'All Things Bright and Beautiful' and there was not a dry eye throughout the Cathedral.

She felt empty inside, almost as if part of her had died with Lisa. She knew that Dan felt the same. As they watched Lisa's coffin being slowly lowered into the ground with a posy of freesias on top of it, they held each other's hands. The foursome now three but just as strong, as she would never leave them completely, Annie was sure of that.

The next few weeks passed in a haze. Richard and Annie were still living at Dan and Lisa's house. They all felt closer to Lisa that way. Annie had started back at the shop part-time and as she finished for the day, she picked up a few stems of freesias. Taking in their heady fragrance, she decided to walk up to her parents' graves. She hadn't been there since her return from Gozo.

Her leg was much stronger now but by the time she arrived at the cemetery, she felt exhausted. Sitting down on a bench, she caught sight of Sidney walking up the path towards her.

"Hello lass. How are you doing?" he sat down beside her.

"I'm real sorry about Lisa. Fine woman."

"Thanks Sidney."

"How's Dan?"

"Not great but he'll get there."

"Aye," nodded Sidney.

The ache in Annie's leg was getting worse, she really

should try to move it but she wanted to ask Sidney a

question that had bothered her for a long time.

"Sidney, can I ask you about Ruby?"

"What about her?"

"Well, I know that she hated yellow roses but you always

buy them for her grave."

"I used to, but I've started buying her favourites again."

"What happened?"

He shifted uncomfortably. "I let my pride get in the way

lass. It took your Lisa to put me back on the right path."

"Lisa?" Annie was surprised at this.

"I went to see her a few weeks ago. You were away on a

trip she said. I took her some flowers and stopped for a bit

of a chat. That's when I told her about the letters."

"What letters were those Sidney?"

"When Ruby passed away, I started to sort out her stuff.

For the charity shops and things like that." He sniffed,

wiping his nose on a pristine white hanky. "As I rooted

through boxes of hers, I came across some letters written

to her by some bloke way back during the war." He

looked at Annie, "They were love letters, all mushy stuff from this bloke."

Annie looked at him questioningly.

"I was courting her at the same time. All the time I was away at war, she was getting letters from some other fellow."

"Did she have any of your letters?"

"Never wrote any!"

Annie smiled, "She picked you though, didn't she."

"That's just what your Lisa said."

Annie felt tears prick her eyes, "What else did Lisa say?"

"She said it's better to have had a true and loyal friendship that you can hold in your heart than to have had nothing at all."

Annie nodded. They made an odd picture, Annie and Sidney sat together on a bench in a graveyard. Sidney patted Annie's hand, "We've both been very lucky lass. We've both been loved by wonderful women. That'll never leave us."

"Yes," Annie smiled, "we've been very lucky indeed."

Printed in Great Britain
by Amazon

55717141R00203